Dear Reader,

I'm really excited to have a book released in 2009, because this year Harlequin celebrates sixty years of producing great books that are loved around the world. A lot has changed for women in that time, but even twenty-first-century women still love being swept away by Harlequin's wonderful modern-day fairy tales.

I've always loved fairy tales. I used to act them out with my grandma and my younger sister when I was a child. Granny was always the wicked witch or the woodcutter. My poor sister was only ever allowed to be a dwarf or an ugly relation of some sort. As older sibling, I claimed the right to be the heroine—the princess. (Sorry, sis!) Cinderella was one of my favorites. Rags to riches, falling in love with a handsome prince—what's not to like?

Just as Cinderella does, Alice in *Invitation to the Boss's Ball* has the most fabulous pair of shoes. I would literally love to strut around in them for a while. What a pity she doesn't believe she's princessy enough to wear them—that is, until she meets the yummy Cameron!

This book is my modern-day take on the classic Cinderella story. It has a downtrodden heroine, a suitably remote and regal prince, and it even has versions of the ugly sisters and the fairy godmother—who actually waves a wand at one point. See if you can spot it!

Love and hugs,

Fiona Harper

—

FIONA HARPER

Invitation to the Boss's Ball

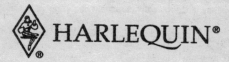

TORONTO • NEW YORK • LONDON
AMSTERDAM • PARIS • SYDNEY • HAMBURG
STOCKHOLM • ATHENS • TOKYO • MILAN • MADRID
PRAGUE • WARSAW • BUDAPEST • AUCKLAND

Recycling programs
for this product may
not exist in your area.

ISBN-13: 978-0-373-17612-0

INVITATION TO THE BOSS'S BALL

First North American Publication 2009.

Printed in U.S.A.

As a child, **Fiona Harper** was constantly teased either for having her nose in a book or for living in a dream world. Things haven't changed much since then, but at least in writing she has found a use for her runaway imagination. After studying dance at university, Fiona worked as a dancer, teacher and choreographer, before trading in that career for video-editing and production. When she became a mother she cut back on her working hours to spend time with her children, and when her littlest one started preschool she found a few spare moments to rediscover an old but not forgotten love—writing.

Fiona lives in London, but her other favorite places to be are the Highlands of Scotland and the Kent countryside on a summer's afternoon. She loves cooking good food, and adores anything cinnamon-flavored. She still can't keep away from a good book or a good movie—especially romances—but only if she's stocked up with tissues. She knows she will need them by the end of the story, be it happy or sad. Her favorite things in the world are her wonderful husband, who has learned to decipher her incoherent ramblings, and her two daughters.

For my grandmother, Alice Johnson,
who always encouraged me to daydream, and
helped make some of my early ones become reality.

CHAPTER ONE

THE old oyster-coloured satin had the most wonderful texture—smooth, but not slippery like modern imitations, stiff and reassuringly heavy. Anyone who saw the cocktail dress would just itch to touch it—and that was what Alice did, letting her fingertips explore it fully, lingering on the crease of the sash as it folded into a bow just under the bustline. This wasn't just a dress. It was a piece of history—a work of art.

She placed it carefully on a padded floral hanger, then hooked the hanger on a rickety clothing rail at the side of the market stall. The next item she took out of the crate was totally different but just as fabulous: a black seventies maxi skirt—a good label—with velvet pile deep and soft enough to get lost in and just not care.

'We're never going to get the stall set up if you don't get a move on.'

She looked up at her best friend and soon-to-be business partner Coreen.

Today Coreen looked as if she'd stepped right out of the pages of a nineteen-fifties ad for washing machines or toasters. She wore a red and white polka-dot dress with a full skirt, her dark hair was coiled into a quiff at the front, and a bouncy ponytail swished at the back as she carefully arranged gloves, little beaded evening bags and shoes on the velvet-draped trestle table that made up the main part of Coreen's Closet—vintage clothing stall *par excellence*.

In comparison, Alice looked positively ordinary. Like many of the other market traders, she'd gone for warmth and comfort over style. Her legs, as always, were covered in denim, and an old, battered pair of trainers graced her feet. Coreen had already made fun of the oversized bottle-green fleece she'd stolen from one of her older brothers. Okay, so she wasn't the epitome of style, but she didn't stand out either. She *was* ordinary. Completely average. No point trying to kid anyone any different.

'Hey, Gingernut!'

Alice sighed and looked up to find the man that everyone at Greenwich market knew only as 'Dodgy Dave' grinning at her.

'Cheer up, love. It might never happen!' he said in his usual jolly manner.

Too late. It already had. Exactly six weeks and two days ago. Not that she was going to tell Dodgy Dave all about her broken heart.

'I wasn't… I was just…'

She waved a hand. Ugh—who cared? It was easier to play along than to explain. She beamed back at Dave, and he gave her a thumbs up sign and carried on wheeling his stash of 'antiques' to his stall.

Okay, there was one thing about her that wasn't ordinary—her hair. And though that sounded as if it was a good thing, it really wasn't. Some people were kind and called it red. The more imaginative of her acquaintances had even tried to say Titian or auburn with a straight face. The fact was it was just plain ginger.

Coreen snapped her fingers in front of Alice's face, and when Alice had focused on her properly she realised Coreen was giving her one of her looks.

'You're not still mooning around over that useless Paul, are you?'

Thanks, Coreen.

Just for a few moments she'd lost herself in the texture and colours of these wonderful old clothes, but Coreen's blunt reminder had brought her back to earth with a bump. 'We only broke up just over a month ago. A girl is allowed to lick her wounds, you know.'

Coreen just snorted. 'I can't believe you didn't dump him first, after the whole kebab incident. I would have done.'

Alice sighed, regretting the fact she'd ever told Coreen about the disastrous evening when she'd got all dressed up to go out to dinner—she'd actually worn a *dress*—only to discover that Paul's idea of a treat was a new computer game and a greasy doner kebab. He'd flung the paper-wrapped kebab in her direction as he'd helped her nerdy flatmates set up the games console. It had landed in her lap and left an unsightly grease stain on the brand-new dress. And he hadn't even noticed when she'd disappeared into the bathroom for twenty minutes, cross with herself for welling up over something so stupid.

At least Paul had *tried*. How could he have known that she'd been hoping for a romantic dinner rather than a boys' night in? She'd never complained before.

But, still....

Okay, she hadn't expected him to roll up in a limo and give her the princess treatment. But being treated like a *girl* for once might have been nice.

'No wonder your luck with men is so awful,' Coreen said

as she pulled on a suede coat with a fur collar. 'You should have "welcome" tattooed on your stomach, because you practically lie down and invite guys to walk all over you.'

Alice didn't look at Coreen. She craned her neck to look at one of the entrances to the market. It was just short of eleven on a Thursday morning—not their busiest day of the week, but someone had to stop and browse soon, surely? Hopefully, that would take Coreen's mind off lecturing her.

'I do not invite men to walk all over me,' Alice said in a quiet but surprisingly defiant tone, well aware that Coreen would have no trouble kicking just about any man into line with her pillar-box red patent peep-toes wedges. Vintage, of course.

Coreen cocked her head to one side. Her curls bounced. 'You *so* do.'

It was no good. Coreen would never get it. She was vivacious and sassy with a glint in her eye and a wiggle in her walk that could stop traffic. Alice knew that for a fact, because she'd once witnessed that same wiggle cause a minor collision down Greenwich High Street. Coreen didn't know what it was like to be as interesting to men as last year's wallpaper.

And, while Paul had not been Coreen's cup of tea, Alice had thought he was lovely. A little bit too into his computer games, and not one for grand gestures, granted, but she'd really liked him. She'd even thought she might have been on the verge of falling in love with him. How stupid. All the time he'd been pining for his ex-girlfriend, and had ended up going back to her. All Alice had fallen into was moping around at home, eating chocolate and feeling rejected and foolish.

'Sometimes when you're in a relationship you have to be prepared to compromise,' she said, hoping desperately that one of the other regular stallholders would wander over for a chat now they were all set up.

No, Alice was a realist. Men weren't even going to press slightly harder on their brake pedals when she walked down the street, let alone swear undying love or promise to bring her all her dreams on a silver platter. But maybe she'd find a nice guy to settle down with eventually.

She frowned. No, 'settle' wasn't the right word. It made it seem as if she *wanted* to settle—which she didn't. She still had dreams. But maybe they weren't as glitzy as the next girl's. Prince Charming could keep his castle and his fairy kingdom. Alice would be happy with an average Joe who just wanted an average Jill to share his life with.

But how did she explain all of that to quirky Coreen, who not only expected but demanded all-out devotion from the men in her life?

'Hey.' An arm came round her shoulders and she smelled Coreen's lavender perfume. 'Just don't forget that even though relationships need compromise, it shouldn't be just *you* doing all the compromising—okay?'

That sounded fine in theory, but no man was ever going to be bowled over by her looks. And if you didn't have looks, you needed a great personality to make a good first impression. Alice didn't think she did too badly in that department, but she was a little shy, and it took her time to relax around people she didn't know and let them get to know her properly. And not many of the guys she met were willing to sit around and hang on a girl's every word unless she had the *looks*. Basically it was a vicious circle Alice had no part in.

But she had discovered one weapon in her arsenal when it came to interacting with members of the opposite sex. One she'd stumbled upon quite by accident…

Somewhere around her fourteenth birthday she'd discovered she'd suddenly become invisible to the male species.

They'd all been too busy being at the mercy of their hormones and drooling after girls who had more, should she say, *obvious* appeal. But Alice had worked out a way to be around guys. She'd become one of them. Almost.

It hadn't been hard. Somehow she'd never got the hang of doing all those unfathomable, girly things that tied teenage boys' brains in knots and drove them insane. So, while she was busy being their buddy, boys got to know her. And when the divas dumped them, they asked her out instead. It hadn't really been a grand plan. Just a pattern she'd noticed and hadn't done anything to discourage.

All her ex-boyfriends had said they liked her calm, straight-forward nature. 'You're so easy to be with,' they'd said, and had laughed about how they'd raced around like headless chickens trying to live up to their previous girlfriends' whims and finally exhausted themselves.

Men didn't have to walk on eggshells around her. She could be friends with them. And friendship was a solid base for something more permanent. The 'obvious' girls might be good for the short term, but when it came to the long haul Alice knew other qualities came into play. Qualities she had in spades—loyalty, honesty, supportiveness.

She turned to look at Coreen. Okay, Paul maybe hadn't been The One after all, and it probably *was* time to look forward to the future, concentrate on her work instead of her love life.

'Believe me, Corrie, I'm not mooning around about anything other than these clothes.'

Coreen grinned and clapped her on the back. 'That's the spirit! But you can't daydream about every piece you hang up, you know.' She took the skirt from Alice and slung it on a hanger. 'And it's a good idea not to fall too much in love with the stock. Yes, it's fabulous, but when someone comes and pays cold hard cash for it I'll be waving each piece bye-bye with a smile on my face.'

Alice nodded. She knew Coreen was right. This was a business—a business she was on the verge of buying into. But falling in love with the clothes was what it was all about, surely? It couldn't hurt to just... *flirt* with them a little, could it?

'We've got a business to run,' Coreen said, her eyes narrowing slightly.

Alice shrugged. 'Technically—until we get the money together for a lease on a shop—*you've* got a business to run. Until then I'm not your partner. I'm just moonlighting from my "proper" job, as my dad calls it.'

Coreen made a dismissive little snort and Alice smiled. That was what she loved about her one-of-a-kind friend. Only Coreen would consider hauling second-hand clothes around the markets of south-east London a proper job, and Alice's home-grown IT consultancy a waste of time.

Actually, Alice's 'proper' job was coming in rather handy at present. Not only was she able to set her own hours, leaving her free to help Coreen out and learn the vintage clothing business, but some of the small companies she did computer troubleshooting for paid her nicely for being at their beck and call. All her spare cash was going into the start-up fund for their dream—Coreen's Closet in bricks and mortar, with a stockroom and a small office. A place where Gladys and Glynis, the two battered mannequins that Coreen had rescued from a skip, could stand in the warm and dry, safe from the danger of being toppled by blustery autumn winds.

At that moment, another gust blew through the market. Although they were in a courtyard with a corrugated roof, surrounded by small shops, Greenwich market was basically an open-air affair, and the wind still whistled through the access alleyways and pillared entrances. Alice pulled her scarf tighter around her neck, and Coreen pulled her coat around her and stamped her feet. Braving the elements was part of the life of a market trader, even if you dealt in old furs and satins, so all in all it was a very ordinary day—and Alice was totally unprepared for what happened next.

Coreen had been to an estate clearance the day before, and had brought back some truly amazing pieces, obviously hoarded by a woman whose children didn't see the designer labels she'd tucked away in the back of her wardrobe as a useful part of their legacy. Some people were like that. They could only think of vintage fashion as wearing other people's clothes, and would never see the inherent beauty of the pieces they were on the verge of throwing away or cutting up for rags.

The satin cocktail dress and the velvet skirt were only part of that haul. Alice carefully lifted a peacock-blue taffeta evening cape out of the box, and when she saw what was underneath it she froze. There they were, just sitting there— the perfect pair of shoes.

She'd been on a steep learning curve about the history of fashion since she'd first met Coreen, but she knew enough to date this pair of evening sandals somewhere in the early fifties. They were the softest black suede and hardly worn. They were elegant, plain—apart from a small diamanté buckle on one side—with a slingback strap. But it was the heels that made the shoes unique. They were totally transparent. Not dull, cheap plastic, though. They were hard and solid, and reflected the light like glass.

Alice hardly dared touch them, they were so beautiful, but she picked one up gingerly and showed it to Coreen.

Her friend nodded in agreement. 'Fabulous, aren't they? I swear, if I was a smaller size, I'd have swiped them for myself.'

Alice peeked at the label. 'But they say they're a five and a half—you're only a smidge bigger than that. Are you sure you don't want them?'

Coreen shook her head. 'American sizing. That's a size four to you and me.'

Size four? Really?

That was it, then. This was destiny.

They were the sort of thing a twenty-eight-year-old *should* be wearing on a regular basis—not canvas sneakers and the big, clumpy things that made Coreen tut.

'They're mine,' she whispered.

Coreen was looking at her again, this time with an understanding light in her eyes.

'How much?' Alice asked.

The ponytail bounced violently as Coreen shook her head. 'I only paid fifty quid for the whole box, and I can sell the rest of the contents for five times that. You have them.'

'Really?'

Coreen winked. 'Really. I know that look. That's the look of a girl who's fallen completely in love and is never going to fall out again. Go on—try them on.'

Even though the stall was only half set up, Alice couldn't wait. She sat on the collapsible chair behind the main table and pulled off her ratty old trainers and thick woolly socks. She didn't even notice the cold on her toes as she took a deep breath and slid her foot into the right shoe, praying fervently that Coreen was correct about the sizing.

Oh, my.

Her first instinct had been right. They were perfect. The shoe moulded to her foot as if it'd been crafted especially for her, and when she slipped the other one on and pulled up the legs of her jeans to get a better look, she gasped. Somehow the shoes made her skinny little ankles and feet look all curvy and shapely and sexy.

She looked up at Coreen. 'The heels? What are they made of?'

Coreen bent forward as Alice twisted her foot to give her a better look. 'Lucite. It's a type of perspex. Really fashionable in the fifties—and not just for shoes. I think I might have a pair of gold-coloured Lucite earrings in my treasure trove.' She indicated the glass-topped wooden display box full of costume jewellery on the other end of the stall. 'But the things to look out for are the handbags.'

'Handbags?' Alice looked shocked. 'Made out of *this* stuff?'

Coreen nodded. 'Cute little boxy things with hinged handles. They come in all shapes and colours and they are really collectible—mainly because a lot of them haven't survived undamaged. In good condition, they can go for hundreds of pounds.'

'Wow!'

'Yes, so keep your eyes peeled.'

Coreen went back to setting up the stall, and Alice looked down at her feet and twisted her ankles this way and that. She wasn't a girly girl, and she didn't normally get excited about something as frivolous as shoes, but it was almost a wrench to slip her feet out of the sandals and return them to her hiking socks and trainers.

'That settles it, then,' Coreen said, bustling Alice to her feet and snatching the shoes away so she could pack them up in a box. 'They're yours.'

Cameron Hunter stood facing the plate glass window that filled one side of his office. From seven hundred feet above sea level, this was one of the most spectacular views in London. It was as if the whole city had prostrated itself at his feet.

Although the day had started crisp and bright, pollution had turned the autumn sky hazy, and now the cityscape below was all pale colours, smudged greys and browns. He stared at the silvery water glinting in the docks below.

He should feel like a king.

Most days he did. Head of his own software company before the age of thirty-five. A company he'd started with nothing but a loan he couldn't afford and an idea that had woken him up in the middle of the night.

And now look at him. This building in the heart of Canary Wharf—and his office within it—could be seen all over London. Further, even. Now every day in the south London suburb where he'd grown up the boys who'd bullied him, the ones who'd taunted him mercilessly, could see the proof of how spectacularly they'd been wrong about him when they walked down the street.

Even better, when they got to work and switched on their computers, it was probably *his* innovative software they were running. Not that he'd leased these offices because of that— it had just been a pleasing perk. When Orion Solutions had first moved in here he'd smiled every time he'd glanced out of the window.

But now… Sometimes he felt…

He shook his head. This was nonsense.

The intercom on his desk crackled.

'Mr Hunter?'

He didn't move, not even to twist in the direction of the speaker. His eyes were fixed on a blue patch of sky on the horizon.

'Yes?' He didn't speak loudly. He never spoke loudly. Somehow there was something in the timbre of his voice that just carried. He had no doubt that Stephanie heard every syllable.

'I know you asked not to be disturbed, Mr Hunter, but something urgent has come up.'

Now he turned and stared at the speaker. 'Come and fill me in.'

He stayed where he was and transferred his gaze to the door. He was not a man accustomed to being kept waiting. Not that he was impatient—far from it—but when you were Cameron Hunter people tended to ask how high it would be convenient for them to jump before he'd even thought of demanding anything of the sort.

There was a timid knock at the door and Stephanie peered round it. He motioned for her to come inside, and she stopped as close to the threshold as she could without actually being outside the room. He'd been having trouble finding a new PA since Aimee had left to have babies and devote herself to full-time mothering. He'd offered to double Aimee's salary if she'd stay. He needed her organisational skills here at Orion. But she'd turned him down, damn her.

Aimee wouldn't have crept into the office as if she was scared of him. But Stephanie, just like her three predecessors, jumped every time he spoke. He didn't mind the fact that his staff respected him—were in awe of him, even. In fact it had been something he'd cultivated when his business had grown beyond a handful of employees. It didn't bother him that people thought him remote. He wasn't the kind of boss who chatted about pets and children, and people didn't expect that of him. They expected him to be in charge, to keep their wages and bonuses coming. His staff knew he was dedicated to them and the company, that he was hard-working and that he rewarded loyalty richly. That should be enough. His personal life was out of bounds. He respected his staff enough not to pry into their business, and they in turn afforded him the same courtesy.

Stephanie clasped her hands together in front of her, looking as if she'd really like to bolt but was attempting to anchor herself. Cameron sighed inwardly.

'The Japanese party have rung ahead to say they've been delayed at the airport. They've asked if we could push the meeting back to three o'clock.'

He nodded. 'Fine. Make the arrangements, would you?'

She gave a hasty nod and sidled round the half-open door.

He walked back to his desk. Before he sat down, he ran his fingertips over the flat, square and now empty jewellery box sitting next to the phone. Until very recently there'd been at least one woman in his life who hadn't quivered with fear when he'd walked into the room. Far from it.

Jessica Fernly-Jones. High society darling and professional butterfly.

She was the woman every red-blooded male in London was dying to have on his arm. And for a while she'd been his. His triumph, his coup.

She'd made him dance through hoops before she'd consented to date him regularly. Not that he'd cared. It had all been part of the game—part of the sacrifice to win the prize. And there was always a sacrifice if something was worth having. When she'd finally relented and agreed to go out to dinner with him, he'd relished the looks of envy and awe on other men's faces as he'd walked through the restaurant with her. It had been even better than when he'd dated a supermodel.

But after two months the hoop-jumping and game-playing hadn't relented, as he'd expected. And he'd started to wonder whether one woman really was worth all the aggravation.

His answer had come the night he'd given her the jewellery box. Lesser women would have squealed and gone all dewy-eyed when they saw the logo of a rather exclusive jewellers on the box. But, give Jessica credit, she'd merely raised an eyebrow and given him a sexy smile. A smile that said she'd knew she'd deserved it, that she was worth every carat the box contained—probably more.

She'd prised open the lid and her eyes had roved the contents of the box.

It had been a diamond pendant. Simple. Elegant. Outrageously expensive.

A small pout had squeezed Jessica's lips together. 'It's lovely, Cameron,' she'd said. 'But don't you remember? It was the *pink* diamond I wanted—not a boring old white one. You *will* be a darling about this, won't you?'

At that moment Cameron had known suddenly and unequivocally that he wouldn't be a darling about anything for Jessica any more. Still, there had been no need to make a scene. They'd gone out to dinner, and he'd explained it all quite carefully before Jessica had flounced off.

Now he had his own little empire he supposed he would need a woman to stand by his side, someone to share all this bounty with. On the climb up he'd always imagined she'd be someone exactly like Jessica. Now, though...

Instead of sitting down he turned round and walked back to the window.

The view was starting to bore him. Just as well he'd be changing it soon.

'Alice? Alice Morton?'

Alice's hand closed around a pound coin in her money belt. She hadn't heard that voice in years. She looked up to find a stylishly dressed woman with a wavy blonde bob smiling at her.

'Jennie? I can't believe it!'

It looked as if Jennie's trademark stripy legwarmers of a decade ago had finally been declared a fashion no-no, because the woman in front of her oozed sophistication. However, there was no mistaking Jennie's bright smile and the aura of excitement she carried with her wherever she went. In a flash Alice had scooted round the velvet-draped stall and the two women launched themselves into a rib-crushing hug.

A polite cough from Alice's left reminded her of what she'd been doing just seconds before Jennie had arrived. She handed the customer she'd been serving her change.

'I'm so sorry! Here you go.'

The woman shrugged and wandered off, with a genuine 'Choose Life' T-shirt in her shopping bag.

Coreen braced her hands on the stall and leaned forward, her eyes practically out on stalks. 'Who's this? Long-lost sister?'

'Almost,' Jennie said, as she and Alice smiled at each other. 'I was engaged to Alice's brother for a couple of years. The fact I didn't get to be Alice's sister-in-law was the thing that made me the saddest when we broke up,' she said.

'Anyway, what are you doing selling vintage lace and platform shoes? The last I heard your IT consultancy was just getting off the ground.'

'Oh, I'm still doing that. It helps pay the bills. In fact, that's how I met Coreen…' She paused briefly to introduce the two women properly. 'When Coreen started selling her stock online a few years ago, she decided to upgrade her system. I sorted her out with what she needed.'

'That doesn't explain how you've ended up selling Wham! T-shirts on a chilly Thursday morning rather than hooking up cables to PCs,' Jennie said to Alice.

Just at that moment another customer walked up and asked Coreen something in-depth about alligator handbags. As she talked to the woman, Coreen made shooing motions with her hands. Bless Coreen! Alice mouthed her a silent thank-you and guided Jennie away from the stall, so they could walk and talk, browsing the clothing and arts and crafts stalls and catching up on over ten years' worth of gossip. She filled Jennie in on what the family were doing now, and she seemed genuinely interested in what Alice had been up to since she'd known her as a shy sixth-former. Alice gave her a potted history—there really wasn't that much to tell—and finished up with how she'd fallen in love with vintage clothes herself after getting friendly with Coreen.

'We're saving hard so we can open up our own vintage clothes boutique,' she said as she finished off.

Jennie smiled at her. 'That'll be just fabulous,' she said, nodding her head, and then she pressed her lips together and looked skywards. 'Tell you what, when you finally open your shop give me a call—I'll organise a launch party that will put you firmly on the map.'

'A party?'

Jennie reached into a soft leather handbag the colour of clotted cream—the stitching on it was fantastic, and screamed quality. She pulled out an elegant business card and handed it to Alice.

'You're an event planner?'

Alice couldn't have thought up a better job for Jennie if she'd tried.

Jennie nodded. 'Isn't it a scream? I get paid to have fun!' She sighed. 'Actually, sometimes the "planning" bit of event planning is a bit of a drag. That's why I'm down here at the market this morning—hunting for inspiration.' She gazed at a stall filled with home-knitted baby cardigans. 'Did you ever meet my stepbrother?'

Alice blinked. Okay—swift change of subject, but she could keep up. She'd heard a lot about the stepbrother during the years Jennie had gone out with Patrick, but he'd been away at university for much of the time they'd been together.

'Tall?' She resisted adding *skinny*, mainly because she hated being described that way herself. 'With glasses?'

Jennie laughed. 'Yes! That was Cam back then. He hasn't shrunk any, but he's lost the specs.'

A flood of memories entered Alice's head and she smiled gently. She'd met Cam—Cameron—just once or twice, the most memorable occasion being at a Christmas do at Jennie's parents' house. She'd been living in fear that she'd get picked next for charades, and had sneaked into Jennie's father's study to hide. She'd almost jumped out of her skin when she'd found a tall, lanky young man sitting in an armchair with a book. He hadn't said anything—just raised an eyebrow and nodded at the other chair.

They'd spent a couple of hours like that, reading quietly, chatting occasionally, until Jennie had discovered them and dragged them out again to join the 'fun'. They'd both pulled a face at the same time. Then he'd smiled at her, and she'd smiled back, and just like that they'd become co-conspirators.

The details of their conversation that evening were fuzzy in her memory, but she hadn't forgotten his smile—or his eyes. Dark brown, streaked with warm toffee, like the tiger's eye stones in a bracelet she'd inherited from her grandmother. What a pity those eyes, with all that warmth and intelligence, had been hidden behind a pair of rather thick, ugly glasses.

'I remember him,' she said quietly. 'He was nice.'

More than nice. But he'd been older. And she'd been sixteen, and still a little terrified of boys she wasn't best buddies with. But that hadn't stopped her wishing it had been

New Year's Eve instead of Christmas Eve, just in case he'd been in need of an available pair of lips when midnight struck.

'Well, he's driving me nuts at the moment, because his company is doing up some old building and he wants—and I quote—a "*different*" opening bash. Something distinctive, he says.' Jennie gave a little huff, as if she were offended that anyone would think she would do anything less.

They'd come full circle, and were now standing next to Coreen's stall again. Jennie reached out and lightly touched the bow on the front of the sixties cocktail dress. 'This really is exquisite,' she murmured.

'Try it on,' Coreen said brightly. 'I've got a deal going with Annabel, who runs the posh children's clothes shop over there. She lets me send customers across to use her changing cubicles as long as I give her first dibs on any gold lamé that comes in.'

Jennie bit her lip.

'Go on—you know you want to,' Alice said. 'The dress is lovely, but you need to see if it works for you. Things that look great on the hanger can suddenly look all wrong once you get them on.'

'And sometimes,' butted in Coreen, 'you find something that's—oh, I don't know—more than the sum of its parts. Like somehow you and the dress combine through some kind of synergy to create... well, a *vision*...'

Alice smiled, glad to see that Coreen wasn't as oblivious to the magic of her stock as she claimed to be. Jennie disappeared with the dress into the ultra-white, minimalist decor of Annabel's emporium.

'Just you wait!' Coreen punched Alice lightly on the arm. 'One day you'll put a dress on and it will happen to you. You'll see!'

Alice imitated one of Coreen's little snorts. 'Yeah, right. Like *that's* ever going to happen.'

Coreen shook her head. 'You'll see…'

There was only one way to deal with Coreen when she got like this: agree, in a roundabout way, and then change the subject quickly. Alice started off gently. 'You're right about some dresses looking magical…'

Pretty soon she'd managed to steer the conversation on to the fashion shows the vintage clothes-sellers staged each year, to advertise their spring and autumn 'collections'. They were always a huge success, and Coreen had heaps of tales about amateur models, slippery-soled shoes and fragile vintage stitching. It wasn't long before they were giggling away like a pair of schoolgirls.

All laughter stopped when they realised Jennie had emerged from Annabel's shop and was staring at herself in the full-length mirror Coreen always placed next to her stall.

'Wow!' both Alice and Coreen said in unison.

It was stunning. The pale colour complemented Jennie's skin tone perfectly, and the skilful tailoring accentuated all her curves. Somehow the dress made her look positively translucent.

An elbow made contact with Alice's ribs. 'Told you,' Coreen said. 'That's *her* dress.'

Okay, perhaps Coreen had a point. But it wasn't hard to look fabulous if you had a figure like Jennie's. She was tall and slim, and she swelled and curved in all the right places. Finding a dress that did that for someone who had more angles than curves, and no chest to speak of at all, would be nothing short of a miracle.

Jennie twirled in front of the mirror. 'I don't care how much it is,' she said, striking pose after pose and never once taking her eyes off her reflection. 'I *have* to have it.'

Coreen grinned and high-fived Alice as Jennie glided away to get changed. When she arrived back at the stall she had a thoughtful look on her face.

'I couldn't help overhearing what you were saying earlier—about the fashion shows, that is.' She looked from Alice to Coreen and back again. 'I've got a proposition for the both of you. And, if I am right about this, this idea could put you well on the way to owning that shop you're after.'

CHAPTER TWO

ALICE sat on the edge of her bed and gazed at the one good photo she had of her and Paul together. One word echoed round her head.

Why?

Why hadn't she been good enough for him? Why had he gone back to Felicity when by all accounts the old trout had made his life a misery by being the ultimate high-maintenance girlfriend?

'Alice,' he'd said, 'you're such a relief after her.'

Relief.

At the time she'd been too caught up in the first flush of a new relationship to be anything but flattered. Now his words just stung.

Her nose was running badly enough for her to give in and sniff. She had promised herself she wouldn't cry any more. She was made of sterner stuff than that.

A phone started to ring. Probably the one in the hall. It rang on.

Alice blew her nose.

It still rang.

'Al-lice!' It was one of her housemates. She shared a house

with the two biggest geeks on the planet. The untidiest geeks too. Roy and Matthew were no doubt on their brand new games console, occupied with slaying aliens and zombies and saving the universe. There was no way they would shift themselves unless their thumbs had locked up and they'd gone cross-eyed. She swiped her eyes with the backs of her hands, then ran down the stairs into the hall and grabbed at the phone before this very persistent person hung up.

'Hello?' she said, not a little breathless.

'Can I speak with Alice Morton?' a male voice said.

Alice's heart began to hammer a little. That was one sexy voice. Deep and warm.

'Hello?' he said again.

'Hi…yes…sorry. This is Alice.' She winced. Compared to The Voice, she sounded all silly and schoolgirlish.

There was a brief pause, and then he spoke again. 'It's been a long time, Alice.'

Was it her imagination, or had his voice got just a little bit softer and warmer—almost as if he were smiling?

'Erm…who is this?'

Please don't let it be a prank caller. Just for a few seconds she'd had the giddy feeling that a man was actually interested in talking to her, in hearing what she had to say. And if this turned out to be a huge joke it would make her life unbearably pathetic. Which was actually quite an accomplishment at this present moment.

'It's Cameron Hunter.'

Cameron? She didn't know anyone called—oh.

'Jennie's step-brother…' he added. 'Didn't she tell you to expect my call?'

Realisation hit Alice like a bolt of forked lightning. Of *course*! The voice was deeper, and more mature, but all of a sudden she recognised the quiet precision, the slight edge of dry humour.

'Oh, of course. Erm…hi, Cameron.'

Blast. Jennie *had* warned her that Cameron would be calling some time soon. According to his stepsister, he was a bit of a control freak, and if they wanted him to agree to the idea that they'd hatched with Jennie for this new building launch party of his, either Alice or Coreen would have to pitch it to him. Alice had begged Coreen to do it—after all, she had all the experience—but Coreen had refused, saying Alice and Cameron had prior history. Alice had argued that reading books on the opposite side of a room from each other while their tipsy families had embarrassed themselves could hardly constitute a 'history', but Coreen would not be budged.

'You're right,' she said, finding her voice had gone all soft and girly. 'It *has* been a long time.'

'Almost twelve years.'

Wow. He hadn't even taken a few seconds to work it out— he'd just remembered. Not many people remembered things about her. Mostly because she kept her head down and kept herself to herself. If it wasn't for her hair she'd be instantly forgettable.

Alice had been staring at the textured glass on the front door while she'd been listening to Cameron. Now she turned around and wandered off in the direction of the kitchen.

Jennie had obviously pitched her idea to him, and now *she* was going to have to convince him to agree to it. The plan had all seemed so stunningly brilliant when she and Coreen and Jennie had hashed it out over drinks last Thursday. The three of them had bounced ideas around, waved their hands in the air, and generally talked over the top of each other for most of the evening.

But now she was on her own, without the benefit of a couple of cocktails inside her, she suddenly realised there were gaping holes in her knowledge of the project. Like what Cameron Hunter's company actually *did*.

There was no point trying to blag her way through this. The Cameron she remembered was too sharp for that, and besides, blagging was a foreign language to her. Maybe when all this was over she'd have to get Coreen to give her lessons. She had a feeling it might come in handy in her future career.

'Jennie said your company is computer-related?' Might as well get the facts straight before she dug herself an even bigger hole. And she might find some common ground.

'Trust my darling stepsister to be a little sketchy with the details. She's normally very efficient, but recently…well, she's been somewhat distracted. Just so you know, my company produces software.'

'And how's it going? I know myself that starting up your own business can be hard. Are you doing okay with it?'

She *heard* him smile. 'Yes, I'd say I'm making ends meet.'

'Good for you!' she said brightly. Oh, dear. That had sounded all fake and patronizing, and she hadn't meant it to be that way at all. She entered the large kitchen she shared with the boys and flicked on the light, hoping that Cameron would take the comment in the spirit it had been meant.

It was time to turn the conversation to something more solid—something she couldn't put her foot in. 'What exactly has Jennie told you so far?' she said.

'Not much. I don't know what's got into her lately—she's been disappearing for hours at a time and being very mysterious. It's more than I can manage to get any sense out of her.'

There was a gentle huff and Alice smiled, knowing how infuriating her own siblings could be.

'She phoned me up and yabbered away at me about a ball and jazz bands and a show-stopping highlight to the evening.' Cameron said in a dry tone. 'I got the impression that bit had something to do with you. Jennie tells me you're some kind of fashion guru these days?'

She'd just been about to perch herself on one of the high stools by the breakfast bar, and she almost burst out laughing and very nearly missed plonking her bottom on the seat of the stool. Alice Morton a fashion guru? Hah!

She almost said as much, but an image of a scowling Coreen flashed across her mind and she quickly changed tack. She was supposed to be inspiring confidence in her abilities as a vintage fashion retailer, not ridiculing her new choice of career. The PR this job would generate for Coreen's Closet could be priceless.

'I see what you mean about Jennie being sketchy with the details,' she said, and then proceeded to give him a potted history of Coreen's Closet. When she'd finished he didn't say anything for a few seconds.

His voice held a hint of surprise when he answered. 'I would never have guessed you would have chosen that as a profession.'

Alice opened her mouth to tell him about the IT work, then closed it again. She kind of liked the fact she'd surprised him, and she decided she wasn't about to kill the first little hint of mystery anyone had ever held about her. She was going to enjoy this while it lasted.

'Well, I think if you love something you should pursue it, no matter the cost.'

That was her new motto. Starting right now. No more distractions. She was going to stop moping about Paul and throw herself into her work. At least with the vintage clothes business it was work she actually liked.

'My thoughts exactly.'

Just for a split second Alice sensed a common bond, a feeling she and Cameron were both wired the same way. The sensation was so strong she wondered if he felt it too. This was how it had been when they'd been younger. Even though he'd been nearly six years older than her, they'd just clicked.

'So, this is what we envisage for the launch party...'

Alice had been folding and unfolding the corner of a takeaway menu, and now she flattened it with her free hand and tucked it between the salt and pepper shakers, removing the distraction.

Jennie had told Coreen of her plans for a lavish ball to celebrate the opening of Cameron's new premises—the fact that the building was 'old' and 'a bit different' was all Alice had been able to get out of her. Jennie had been struggling to come up with something to set the evening apart, something that encapsulated the idea of new and old coming together, and then she'd overheard Coreen and Alice's conversation about the market fashion shows and she'd made a connection.

Cameron wanted something that spoke of class, success, elegance. And what could pull all these things together better than a unique charity fashion show, full of the glamour and romance of a bygone age, but showing how vintage clothes could add individuality and style to a twenty-first century wardrobe? And if they sold the idea to Cameron, Coreen's Closet were going to supply and source the clothes. Alice explained all of this to him, and as she talked she forgot she was selling a business idea and just rambled on about the glorious clothes, the icons of yesteryear, and how everyone who attended it would feel as if they'd stepped back into a magical time.

Cameron listened. He said 'mmm-hmm' and 'okay' quite a few times as she outlined the plan to auction the clothes off as the show progressed. But she knew that they weren't the normal noises of a man who was pretending he was listening when he was really thinking about last night's game. She knew he was taking it all in, capturing every detail with his quick mind and mentally sorting it all.

'I presume, from what you've told me about the history of your new business venture, that you and your partner aren't just going to be giving the clothes away? How does the charity angle work?'

'I wish we *could* give them away. However, we've worked out a plan with Jennie. We'd set very reasonable reserve prices on all the pieces—similar to what we'd get if we were selling them one-by-one on the stall. As each piece is auctioned off we'll keep the reserve price, and anything that is bid over that will go to charity.'

'What if the reserve isn't met—or all the clothes only just reach the set figure?'

'Jennie suggested my business partner, Coreen, should be the auctioneer. She's extremely knowledgeable, and believe me, she could sell mink coats to…well, minks.'

A loud and unexpected snort of a laugh erupted from the earpiece of the phone.

'Alice,' he said, his tone still full of warm laughter, 'you always did have a very singular way of looking at things.'

Was that a good thing or a bad thing? Had she just blown it?

'With Coreen doing the talking you'll have more than enough to donate to charity, I promise.'

'If this Coreen is anything like you say she is, I don't doubt it.'

'And Jennie said you'd put in a hefty donation yourself.'

'Did she, now?'

Alice winced. 'Yes.'

Coreen's Closet could handle giving the extra money to one of the local children's charities because they'd be shifting a whole lot of stock in one go—and, even better, they'd be attracting the attention of a lot of well-to-do potential customers. The free publicity would be fantastic. With the extra money in their account, and the press coverage, she and Coreen might just be able to twist the arm of their business manager at the bank to give them a loan for the rest of the capital needed to lease and outfit a small shop.

'If we do this right, this won't just be another party—same drinks, same faces, same canapés. It will be something truly memorable. Each piece of vintage clothing we sell is unique, one of a kind. For those that buy at the auction, every time they wear that jacket or carry that handbag they'll remember your company and *think* one of a kind. Even those that don't buy anything will have their memories jogged when they turn on the TV and catch an old movie, or see a poster in a shop display. They'll be instantly transported back to the elegant and original night when you opened your new offices and your company started a new chapter in its history. And that's what you want, isn't it? For the event to be distinctive, because then it will be remembered.'

Alice had now run out of words, and she had the sense that adding to them with empty silence-fillers would just be a mistake. So she closed her mouth and stared out of the kitchen window into the dark evening sky, waiting for Cameron's response.

Suddenly his good opinion—of her, of her hopes and dreams—mattered. She held her breath.

'Okay, Alice. You've got a deal. I like the idea.'

Alice was very glad Cameron didn't have a video phone,

because she took that moment to do a silent victory dance around the kitchen.

'I understand you're going to liaise with Jennie about the party, and she's going to keep me in the loop. Do you really think you can pull this off in four weeks?'

Alice was tempted to hyperventilate. She was so far out of her depth it wasn't funny. 'Of course,' she said.

'I look forward to seeing you then. Sorry to have interrupted your evening, but I was intrigued by what Jennie had told me and I wanted to find out more immediately. I've always found it helps to put the brakes on before she gets too carried away. Sometimes her ideas just don't pan out. Anyway, I'll let you get back to…whatever you were doing.'

'It's fine. I wasn't really…'

She knew she should just say goodbye gracefully and put the phone down, but she didn't.

'You know, Alice, I always thought you had it in you to surprise everyone.'

That was possibly the nicest thing anyone had ever said to her.

Oh, her clients gushed occasionally about her, but, to be honest, they'd have sainted anyone who could have got their e-mail going again when an IT disaster struck. And not only was Cameron saying nice things, he was saying them in his lovely voice. She could have listened to it all evening.

'Thank you, Cam.'

He chuckled. 'Cam… I don't think anyone but Jennie calls me that any more.'

'Sorry…Cameron.' She frowned. 'What *do* people call you, then?'

'Oh, *Your Highness* pretty much works for me.'

Now it was Alice's turn to laugh.

'See you in four weeks, Alice.'

And then he was gone.

She pulled the phone away from her ear and stared at it. This evening was getting progressively more surreal.

She cradled the phone to her chest as she slipped off the kitchen stool and wandered down the hallway to replace it on its base.

She made her way upstairs and pulled a book off her shelf, intending to read at least five chapters while soaking herself in a very hot bath. And as she threw her clothes onto the bed and pulled on her comfy old dressing gown, the slightly crumpled photo that had been lying face-down on the duvet fluttered to the floor and hid itself under the bed.

'Moon River' chimed from Alice's pocket as her mobile vibrated. In an effort to contort herself into a position whereby she could reach it, she whacked her head on the underside of the desk she'd been crawling under. There was a muffled snicker from somewhere else in the office.

Finally she got her phone to her ear. 'Hello?'

'Hello.'

That one simple word, said in a calm, deep, velvety voice, set Alice's heart-rate rocketing. Why did his voice make her think of log fires and thick hot chocolate?

'Cameron?' Oh, flip. Did that nauseating little squeak of a voice belong to *her*? She cleared her throat.

'Alice, we have a problem.'

We? Had he just said *we*?

'We do?'

She heard a muffled shuffling sound, as if he was pacing around. 'My ridiculous stepsister has decided to…decided to…*elope*! I knew she was acting strangely, but…'

Did modern-day women still elope? Alice wasn't sure. Didn't that only happen to corset-wearing heroines in historical novels? Either way, it was wildly romantic. She drifted off into a little daydream about carriages, hooded velvet capes and moonlight.

However, Cameron's voice sliced through her fantasy. 'No Jennie means no ball. Which means no fashion show.'

That's right. Break it to me gently, Cameron.

Was she mistaken, or was there a hint of imperious displeasure in his tone?

Anyway, the fashion show *couldn't* be off. She and Coreen had already planned what to do with the money. They'd set their hearts on being in a shop by February. Without the income and publicity from the show, they might have to wait until the following year.

Alice thought of the market fashion shows, how all the traders pulled together and made it happen.

'*I* can do it. I can organise the fashion show.'

Had she really just said that? A market fashion show, with people's sisters and cousins as models, was a bit different from the kind of upmarket affair Jennie had been planning.

There was a split-second pause before Cameron said, 'I like your fighting spirit, Alice.'

She didn't have much of a choice, did she?

'We both need this event to be a success,' he said. 'And I agree that bailing out now isn't an option.'

That wasn't *exactly* what she'd meant...

'You'll just have to take over,' he added, almost to himself.

Alice blinked. For a while she'd forgotten where she was. She'd stopped noticing the faded blue carpet and the tangle of wires in every direction. But now she was back in the real world, staring at a bare patch somebody's feet had worn under the desk.

'I beg your pardon?'

'You'll just have to help me. You said you could organise the fashion show part. Couldn't you do the rest too? I'll pay you Jennie's fee.'

He mentioned a figure that made Alice's eyes water. With that sort of capital behind them Coreen's Closet could have its own premises by Christmas, never mind February. It almost made her forget that he hadn't exactly asked nicely.

'But I have no experience of—'

'Neither do I. But I'm prepared to give it a go if you are. We've only got three weeks now, and it's too late to start from scratch with another event planner.' His voice softened. 'Come on, Alice. For our own reasons, we both need to pull this off.'

It didn't matter if Cameron had asked nicely or not. He was right.

'Okay,' she said slowly. 'I'll think about it.'

Cameron obviously decided to take that as a yes, because he started to reel off instructions and bark at her about couriering Jennie's files over.

'Slow down a minute!'

Cameron broke off in mid-flow, seemingly flummoxed by the concept that someone might have something better to do with their time than fulfil his every whim. Alice took advantage of the silence.

'You can't send stuff round right this minute. I'm not at home. I'm at work. I won't be there to sign for it.'

'Oh. Sorry. I should have… But Jennie said you weren't at the market today. I haven't interrupted you on a house visit, in the middle of rifling through someone's wardrobe, have I?'

'No—ouch!' Alice had turned to sit cross-legged on the floor and her head had made contact with the desk once more. 'Actually, I'm rifling through someone's network.'

There was a pause. 'Did you say *network*?'

Alice nodded to herself. 'Jennie really is sketchy on the details, isn't she? I'm an IT consultant by day and a vintage fashion retailer by night. Think of it as my alter ego—my secret identity.'

'Not so secret any more…now that you've told me.'

She grinned. He had a point there. Somehow she knew Cameron was grinning back on the other end of the line. For a few moments neither of them said anything, then Alice shook herself—literally—and decided to get back to business. Perhaps that would stop this slightly light-headed feeling that seemed to be sweeping over her.

'I need to get an idea of what your new offices are like— to make sure what we're planning matches the surroundings. The building is what we'll be there to celebrate, after all, isn't it?'

Just as she'd been able to 'hear' him smile, she now sensed him…what? Gloating?

'You should see it. It's something else—totally unique. An old nineteen-thirties factory on the Isle of Dogs. Classic Art Deco style. All the plant and machinery is gone, but we've done as much as possible to preserve the original features.'

A picture formed in Alice's mind as he talked: geometrical shapes, cool white plaster, long horizontal windows. 'It sounds fascinating. And what about the space for the party? Is there enough room? How big is it? Over how many levels?'

His voice was full of dry humour when he answered. 'And you told me to slow down. One question at a time, Morton.'

But he didn't sound displeased in the slightest. In fact, he addressed her queries one by one in detail, and she could tell from the tone of his voice he was enjoying the chance to talk about his current pet project.

'I mean it. You need to see it, Alice. What are you doing tomorrow?'

Why don't you get to the point, Cameron? Stop beating around the bush.

She frowned. 'I was supposed to be sorting out a—'

'Cancel it.'

Alice spluttered. 'I can't do that! My clients are relying on me.'

'Give me the address and I'll send a team from my own IT department. I'll see to it you won't lose any business because of this.'

It was all very well for Cameron to wave his magic wand and make all her objections disappear, but she wasn't at all sure she wanted a bunch of strangers doing her work for her. But it was that or give up on the whole fashion show idea. And that meant delaying her launch into her new career, which she really wasn't prepared to contemplate now it was almost within her grasp.

And by the way, Mr Hunter...See that mountain over there? You couldn't just tell it to up and jump into the Thames, could you? It's spoiling my view.

She was starting to realise that the focussed, determined young man she'd met all those years ago had matured into a formidable force. And something was bothering her. Something on the fringes of her consciousness.

'Cameron?'

He stopped mid-flow, in the middle of giving her more potted history of his new building. 'Yes?'

'What did you say your company was called?' Now she thought about it, she didn't remember getting down to specifics—she'd been too busy pitching her idea.

'Orion.' He sounded puzzled. 'Didn't Jennie tell you that?'

Alice almost dropped her phone. 'Orion?' she whispered.
'As in *Orion Solutions*?'

'Yes. That's it.'

Very clever.

Hunter...Orion...It all fitted now.

She'd booted up the computer on the desk above her only
a couple of minutes ago. Full of Orion software. Like almost
every other computer on the planet. Suddenly the air in her
office had grown a little sparse. She wanted to open a window
and stick her face outside into the cold air, but she had a
feeling they were welded shut.

Had she just agreed to organise a party for the head of
Orion Solutions—one of the fastest growing software enter-
prises in the world? Boy, she was way out of her league. Way,
way out of her league.

But this was *Cameron*. The young man she'd hidden out
at a Christmas party with.

No, it wasn't working. She couldn't marry the two ideas
together in her head, even though she knew deep down he
must have changed since then. Just talking to him, she sensed
subtle changes. Now it all made sense. He'd always been
reserved and precise. But now when he talked there was an
unmistakable undercurrent of confidence and inner strength
she'd always sensed had been there which now had risen to
the surface. Would he have changed on the outside too?
Twelve years was a long time.

The mental image that thought conjured up was appealing.
She could see a tall, slim man—not gangly and awkward any
more—with the same unruly dark hair that curled past his collar.
His eyes would be the same warm brown, but there would be
more lines round his mouth and at the corners of his eyes.

There was a meaningful cough from beyond the desk.

Alice noticed a pair of pinstriped legs move a few steps closer. Mr Rogers. She'd forgotten all about him.

'I better go,' she mumbled. 'I'll see you tomorrow.'

'I'll meet you at noon.' He reeled off the address of his new headquarters.

As he spoke, she was vacantly staring at a web of cables off to her left. Something drew her attention—some instinct told her to take a closer look. And then she spotted it—the source of all of the solicitors' problems. It was going to be a nasty job to sort out but, hey, 'nasty' normally meant 'time-consuming', and that translated into more cash. Something she was only too glad of.

'Alice? Is that okay?' The deep, rich voice made her jump.

'No...yes...that sounds fine. I'll see you then.'

Cameron rang off with his normal brevity, and Alice crawled over to the knot of cables she'd been inspecting. There was a murmur and a shuffle and the pinstriped legs moved even closer.

'Anything I can do?' a thin voice enquired.

Mr Rogers wasn't being helpful—far from it; he had the air of someone trying to hurry someone else along. Fair enough, since he paid for her services by the hour.

'No, I'm fine,' she said, running her thumb and forefinger along a stretch of wire to check where it disappeared to. 'But I'd love a cup of tea—if you're making one, that is.'

There was a quiet huff, and the legs disappeared out of the office door.

Alice didn't feel guilty about that in the slightest. She'd get much more work done if someone wasn't hovering over her all the time. And she didn't feel guilty about stopping for five minutes to take Cameron's call. If she hadn't been sitting here under the desk, staring at the wires, it would have taken her hours longer to find the source of the problem. She backed out from under the desk, stood up and brushed herself down, pleased to be off her knees and standing tall.

Cameron arrived at the construction site early, keen to meet with the foreman and get an update before he showed Alice around. Although he was required to wear a hard hat, it was hardly necessary as all the major work had been done. Only the finishing touches were being seen to—doors were being hung, sockets were being fixed to the walls and flooring was being laid.

He checked his watch. She'd be here in an hour. He brightened unexpectedly at the thought. Alice had been a nice kid. A little unsure of herself, as teenage girls often were, but kind and intelligent. He was glad to know she'd lost none of that warmth in the intervening years. And she'd certainly seemed full of fire when he'd talked with her on the phone. It was nice to actually converse with someone for a change rather than just give orders.

What was she to him, then? A friend?

He didn't really have many friends. Hadn't really had time for them while he'd worked himself stupid getting where he was today. Most of the men he socialised with fell into one of two categories. They were either colleagues or competitors, and both were apt to put on a false front because they either wanted to impress the boss or they were hoping to get close to him and learn something to their advantage.

And women... Well, women *never* wanted to be just friends with him. They also fell into two camps: tigers and jellyfish. The tigers, like Jessica, were blatant about their attraction to him—and his money. And he obliged them by taking them out to the best spots in London, treating them like royalty... As long as they understood he wasn't looking for anything permanent, wasn't looking for someone to share his throne at present. They were all just *temporary* princesses.

The jellyfish—the second type of woman, like his current PA—trembled and stuttered in his presence. But he saw the glint of attraction in their eyes too—they were just too scared to act on it. Both responses were starting to get on his nerves.

He couldn't pigeonhole Alice into either of these groups, and that made her an unknown species. Intriguing.

She'd been pretty too, in her own way. Beautiful eyes—a fascinating hazel that were one moment green and the next nutty brown. She'd been like an ugly duckling, just on the cusp of becoming a swan. Sometimes, when she'd moved a certain way or changed her expression, he'd had the strangest sense that a glorious, transformed Alice was about to burst through the meek outer shell.

He shook his head.

This was his problem with women. He let his imagination run away with him and started thinking all sorts of ridiculous things. He became dazzled by the *idea* of the woman, and always ended up being disappointed when they didn't live up to the dream. But he'd dated enough gold-diggers now that he could spot them at thirty paces. It didn't stop him taking them out, though. In fact, it suited his whole 'temporary princess' idea. He didn't expect much from the Jessica-types, and therefore he was rarely disappointed. And there was no danger of them leaving a scar when the relationship ended.

When people got too close, they judged. They found all the bits of your psyche you didn't want to acknowledge and held them up in front of your face to see, along with a few more faults you didn't realise you'd had. No, he'd had enough of being judged.

But that really was a moot point these days. He was top dog. *He* did the judging. And if anyone was foolish enough to put him under the microscope they'd only come away with the verdict that he was the best and that he had the best of everything. And that was just what he'd been aiming for all these years.

A tall fence of chipboard panels painted roughly in forest green surrounded the new headquarters to Orion Solutions. The gate was covered with brightly coloured signs warning of all sorts of dire consequences to those who dared step inside. The boundary fence was at least twelve feet high, and this close to it, Alice could see nothing of the building beyond.

Being fairly local, she now realised she remembered the factory in its previous incarnation as a bakery. It had been left almost derelict for more than a decade, and the only details she could recall were broken panes in the wide horizontal windows and a dirty concrete façade.

Now she was actually here, ready to see the site and show her ideas to Cameron, her stomach was churning. Coreen really should have come. She was good at the talking and schmoozing. Alice was good at the practicalities—the behind-the-scenes stuff.

But you didn't need to *schmooze* Cameron on the phone, a little voice inside her head whispered. You talked, he listened. It'll be the same now.

But her stomach didn't seem to believe her head. It was still rolling around as if it was being battered by one of the old kneading machines that had lived in the old bakery.

And Coreen hadn't helped this morning. She'd insisted Alice go round, so she could make sure she was dressed 'fittingly' for a representative of Coreen's Closet. Coreen had taken a single look at Alice's one good trouser suit, tutted, and then dragged Alice into her bedroom. In no time she'd bullied Alice into stripping down to her underwear. Alice had stood there like a shop dummy, being prodded and poked and pinched, and when Coreen had pronounced her ready she'd taken one look in the mirror and flipped out.

She'd looked like Coreen's freaky twin sister, with her hair quiffed and pinned. The floral fifties dress was undoubtedly gorgeous, but Alice's chest didn't fill the darted bodice and the large circular skirt just swamped her. The icing on the cake had been the bright red lipstick.

She'd looked ridiculous. She wasn't that girl—that frilly, sexy, pouting girl. She was Alice. And Alice looked like a big fat fake in that get-up. This time Coreen hadn't been going to get her way. Alice had told her friend so in no uncertain terms, and then she'd reached for a tissue and wiped the lipstick off, leaving a wide red smudge on her cheek.

Once Coreen had got over the shock of being contradicted, she'd set to work again, agreeing that the full-on retro look maybe wasn't for Alice, but a touch of vintage might add a little pizzazz to an otherwise dull department store outfit.

So here Alice stood, the result of makeover number two. Coreen had let her keep the loose-legged chocolate trousers, as she'd said they flattered Alice's shape and made her look like Katherine Hepburn, but she'd replaced the suit jacket with a collarless forties one in deep crimson tweed. Even Alice liked the fake fabric bunch of grapes in autumn colours that adorned the breast. She's brushed out the ridiculous hairstyle and opted for a low, sleek ponytail, and had let Coreen add some lipstick in a berry shade that complemented both the jacket and her colouring.

It would have been madness to tell Coreen—it would only

have made her even more incorrigible—but Alice *did* feel smart and stylish, in a way that was uniquely *her*. At least she did until she reached the tall chipboard gates that barred her entrance to Cameron's building. Now she was tempted to turn and run away on her chunky-heeled boots. She looked back down the road to where she'd parked her car.

'Alice Morton?'

She spun round to find a gruff-looking builder eyeing her up and down through a gap in the gate.

'Yes,' she said, finding her voice unusually croaky.

He nodded towards the construction site. 'This way,' he said, and cracked the gate wider so she could pass through it. 'The boss and some of the architects are inside. I've been told to take you to them. Oh—and you'll need this.'

He jammed a bright yellow helmet on her head. Alice was relieved for the second time this morning that the quiff hadn't stayed. She'd have been digging hair pins out of her scalp for weeks if it had still been there.

She clutched the old school satchel that held her drawings and ideas—Coreen had sworn it would make a funky alternative to a boring old briefcase—and followed the man along a path towards the new Orion building.

And then she looked up and her feet forgot to walk.

Wow.

CHAPTER THREE

CAMERON had said he wanted a 'distinctive' opening celebration, and now she saw why. These types of buildings had been considered ugly and out of fashion until relatively recently—left to crumble or bulldozed and replaced with yet another chrome and glass structure.

The building was a low rectangle, with maybe only three or four storeys—it was difficult to tell where the divisions lay, because the whole width of the building was filled with tall windows with horizontal panes, punctuated by plain white pillars and, in the centre, a fabulously ornate doorway that made her think of Greta Gabo films and Egyptian tombs all at the same time.

Alice seemed to remember the door and its stone and glass surround having been painted a sickly green in days gone by, but now the giant sunburst design that reached to the flat roof was highlighted in glossy black and gold.

She started walking again, trying to take it all in.

The stock of Coreen's Closet had always seemed so glamorous and high-quality to Alice, but in the face of such opulence it suddenly seemed a little...second-hand. Could they *really* pull this off? How did you live up to a building like this?

However, as she got closer, she reminded herself that this building had once been old and tired, and it had only taken someone with a little vision to see past the grimy exterior to the potential underneath. It too was second-hand. And didn't it look fabulous? With this thought in mind, she steeled herself and followed the builder to the main doors.

At least she'd find a friendly face inside—someone she knew she'd be totally comfortable with.

Her guide left her, and she took a moment to smooth down her jacket before she pushed at the door with diagonal glass panels. The entrance hall was dirty and dusty, but clues to its splendour were there if one looked hard enough. The floor was white marble, and she could see a contrasting interwoven border in black at the edges of the space. And, underneath a dust cloth, the corner of what must be the original wooden reception desk was visible—all sleek lines and curves.

Two men in suits—the architects, probably—were standing near a second set of double doors that were reached by three low steps spanning the width of the reception area. The men were deep in conversation, pointing things out to each other on a set of plans. Alice stood in the centre of the space, her feet together, her satchel clasped in both hands in front of her, and looked around to see if she could spot Cameron.

'Alice?'

Her pulse did an odd little leap at the unmistakable rumble of that voice. She twisted round, first to the right and then to the left, to see where it was coming from. The acoustics in this bare space must be a little weird—because it sounded as if he was close by, but he was nowhere to be seen.

She turned to face front again, and noticed one of the architects looking at her. Her pulse did another little syncopated skip, and this time it had nothing to do with nerves at seeing an old acquaintance again or putting her business on the line.

Time stopped and sped up all at the same time. A wave of awareness hit her so hard it was as if she'd run full pelt into a brick wall.

She hadn't paid much attention to the two men when she'd first entered, too intent on locating Cameron, but now the taller of the two had fixed her with a very intense gaze and she was feeling oddly breathless.

And then his mouth moved, and she heard her name on his lips, and everything slowed down even more and became all far away and echoey. She tried to decipher what her senses were telling her, but they were making no sense at all. The log fire and chocolate voice was coming from *that* mouth, from *those* lips...

She began to shake as he walked towards her. But not from fear; this was something totally new—a reflex she'd never known she'd possessed. She'd found men physically attractive before—of course she had—but never this...this... whatever it was.

She wanted to sit down. Or lean against something. Preferably him.

It couldn't be...could it?

As he moved towards her, his hand beginning to reach forward for hers, she studied him, and in the odd little bubble of time she found herself in there was plenty of opportunity to do so. He was still tall, but now he was broad—without being bulky. Gone was the slightly shaggy hair, replaced by a short, neat cut that did wonders for his cheekbones. Was it illegal for a man to have cheekbones that gorgeous? And even though his mouth was hard, and every line in his face an angle, she wanted to reach out and touch him—just to feel the skin, explore the planes and creases. And his eyes…tiger's eyes. Cameron's eyes.

This was Cameron.

Finally her tongue unknotted itself. 'H—Hi.'

She extended her hand to meet his and instantly regretted it. She could feel the trembling all the way up to her shoulders. He took her hand, but instead of shaking it, he merely clasped it and leaned forward—and down, of course—to place a feather-soft kiss on her right cheek.

Alice dropped her satchel.

The bag landed on his rather expensive Italian shoes and Cameron reached down and picked it up. He offered it to Alice. She fumbled with it and finally anchored it in her grasp. A horrible sense of disappointment settled in the pit of his stomach. He'd felt the quivering in her small hand and it meant only one thing. Jellyfish.

Still, he smiled as he gestured for her to follow him. No matter what he felt on the inside, he never let a glimmer of it reach the surface. He'd learned long ago that being that weak cost dearly.

She'd surprised him once again. But this time it hadn't been a nice surprise.

Where was the Alice he'd spoken to on the phone—the woman who was full of bright ideas, enthusiasm and humour?

He gave her the grand tour, showed her the sweeping white staircases with the original black cast iron railings, pointed out the boxy ceiling lamps in opaque glass, the door furniture, the floor-to-ceiling windows. Alice said nothing. Just trotted around after him, taking the odd snap with a slim digital camera. In the end he got sick of the sound of his own voice so he summoned Jeremy, the chief architect, to come and spout facts.

Alice blinked at Jeremy, with those large, changeable eyes of hers, and pulled a small black notebook out of her pocket, occasionally scribbling something in it.

The last stop on the tour was the atrium—the chosen venue for the launch party. In days gone by the factory had had a large courtyard in the centre of the building. Jeremy's firm had suggested changing nothing about the exterior walls, save a little cosmetic work, and had proposed enclosing the long rectangular area with a glass roof, carefully constructed not to ruin the line of the building.

But they didn't enter it at ground level. Cameron wanted her to have the best view, so he led the silent Alice and the chattering architect up to his suite of offices on the top floor. He'd chosen this section of the building as his domain. Soon, instead of looking out of his window and seeing the rest of the world that had yet to be conquered, he would walk out onto a balcony that ran the entire width of his office and see his kingdom: people scurrying this way and that, talking, networking, making plans and creating ideas.

From up on the balcony, overlooking the entire atrium, she'd get a sense of the vastness of the space. If *that* didn't elicit a sentence from her, he didn't know what would.

They entered his office, almost complete now, and Jeremy, who was starting to seriously get on Cameron's nerves, wittered on about the original dark wood panelling and plans for the décor. Cameron silenced him with a look, and led Alice to the double doors in the wall of glass and steel windows and opened them wide.

She gave him a quizzical look, and he stood there on the threshold and watched her walk across the balcony, which was a good twenty feet deep, until she reached the polished brass rail that topped the parapet. For a few seconds she didn't do anything—not even breathe, it seemed to Cameron. Then her ribcage heaved and she turned to face him, her eyes sparkling. Slowly a smile blossomed, stretching her lips wider and wider until she was beaming at him.

Suddenly he realised she hadn't needed to say anything at all. Foolish of him to have required it of her.

He found himself walking to join her, an unplanned smile changing his own features. Silently, they both stared at the empty courtyard, a multi-layered geometric fountain its only feature. It was bone dry at present, but by the night of the ball, it would be bubbling joyously.

She turned to face him. 'This is it?' she asked, her face suddenly alive. 'Is this where the ball is going to be held?'

He nodded.

After a few seconds she returned to staring at the atrium. 'It's perfect,' she whispered, and then she fell silent again, her eyes roving over the long horizontal windows of the offices, the simple elegant lines of the building, the white plasterwork with contrasting black paintwork that somehow seemed anything but stark, with all the light and warmth radiating from the glass roof above, creating shadows and depth.

As Alice studied his building he studied her, discarding his first impressions and looking more carefully.

He could see her mind working, and she ran the fingers of her left hand over the top of her ear in an unconscious gesture, almost as if she was smoothing down her hair under the yellow plastic hat. But her hair was in a ponytail and didn't need tidying. He was glad to see she hadn't hidden her hair colour with dye. He'd never seen anyone with a shade of red hair to match it— not that he'd been aware he'd been making comparisons all these years. It was almost *impossibly* red. So bright he couldn't do anything but stare at it as she concentrated on the view.

Alice wasn't pretty—not in the traditional sense. She didn't have dimples and a cute little nose, big blue eyes or fluttery lashes. But there was an elegance about her, a fragility that was understatedly feminine. Every tiny movement, even the redundant motion of her fingers in her hair, was full of a quiet grace that even the dusting of pale freckles across her nose and cheeks could do nothing to dispel.

No, she wasn't pretty. But she might well be beautiful one day—if she ever chose to grow into it.

'Can we go down? Take a look around?'

There was no trace of timidity in her voice now. Her eyes were full of determination, and he could see the glint of ideas firing in their depths. He led her downstairs, saying nothing, letting her thoughts have room to grow and develop. He didn't like people who chattered uselessly. A fact that Jeremy, who was trailing after them, would do well to remember. As they reached the entrance hall, with its doors onto the courtyard, the architect opened his mouth—probably to say something about the construction of the glass roof—but Cameron waved him away. He wasn't needed any more.

Alice stepped into the atrium and was suddenly energized—almost as if she'd been hit by a bolt of lightning. She walked briskly this way and that, talking nineteen to the dozen, pulling sketches and notes out of her funny little bag, then stuffing them back in again before he'd had a chance to even glance at them.

Inwardly, he grinned. Yes, *this* was what he'd expected from her. This vision. This unbridled enthusiasm. This…passion. Working with Alice Morton wouldn't be a problem—far from it. In fact he had a hunch it might be a real pleasure.

And before he'd even realised quite how it had happened he'd joined her—talking and gesticulating and smiling.

Jeremy, the discarded architect, was standing in the entrance hall watching them—watching Cameron. His eyebrows were halfway up his forehead and he shook his head in total wonderment. If he hadn't seen the transformation in Mr Hunter himself, he'd have never believed it.

There was a large package waiting for Alice when she got home the next evening. She ripped open the plastic bag and discovered a folder stuffed with notes and sketches about the ball.

There was a note in black ink, written on heavy paper in a precise hand. With typical Cameronness, he hadn't bothered with pleasantries and got straight to the point:

> *Alice, here are all of Jennie's notes on the ball. I sent my PA over to Jennie's offices to pack the stuff up and she couldn't make head nor tail of it. Good luck.*
> *Cameron.*

He'd sent his PA? Alice was tempted to laugh. What would it be like to have people snap to attention when you walked into a room, rather than tread on your toes because they hadn't noticed you standing there? Believe it or not, the latter happened to her a lot more than most people realised.

Thankfully, Jennie had obviously been a lot more together on this project than Cameron had thought. There were lists of caterers, with different ones ticked or crossed off, a note of the band that had been booked, the addresses of a number of florists. All in all, it seemed she'd been planning a wonderfully glamorous event, but...

Something was missing. Something to tie everything together.

That was why she and Coreen had been struggling to come

up with a collection of outfits that would work for the show. Over the weekend they'd inspected all their stock thoroughly, teaming up accessories with clothes, putting aside those they knew they wanted for the show. But the outfits they'd ear-marked seemed to have no common thread. Seeing them in-dividually would be great, but if they were to go down a catwalk together it would seem like a total mish-mash.

In short, they needed a theme.

There were pages of scribbles, where Jennie had obvi-ously brainstormed ideas with herself, but she'd come up with nothing solid. In fact there seemed to be an awful lot of doodles of love hearts, wedding rings, and the details of a flight to Las Vegas. Not Alice's dream wedding venue—but each to their own… In recent days, it was obvious Jennie's mind had not been on the job.

Thinking of bright lights and big names, an idea popped into Alice's mind.

Old Hollywood glamour.

A mix of old and new, extravagance and elegance—just like Cameron's wonderful building. And it fitted Jennie's plans for a thirties feel for the evening—she'd already booked a big band and some swing dancers before disappearing over the Atlantic in a haze of true love. Oh, yes. This was *perfect*. She got on the phone to Coreen straight away, and they spent the whole evening in Coreen's lounge sorting through stock.

Now they had an over-arching idea it would be easy to hunt for outfits and place them in collections. Each mini-collection would then make a smaller section of the fashion show. They hatched a plan to show each collection and then auction those pieces off before carrying on with the next one.

Once they started thinking evening wear, day wear, and dif-ferent eras, Alice's love of old movies came in handy and she suggested film title themes for each part of the show. As she and Coreen drank wine and sorted through clothes, they settled on a shortlist of five: *Roman Holiday* would be all printed fifties cottons, full skirts and summer wear. *Some Like It Hot* would show off evening dresses, sequins, tight skirts and high heels. *Pillow Talk* would contain vintage lingerie— corsets, babydoll nightdresses and silk slips that these days many women bought to wear as cocktail dresses. *Casablanca* would be boxy jackets and high-waisted trousers, wool knits and kid gloves. And, last but not least, Coreen's favourite: *Rebel Without a Cause*. She was practically salivating at the thought of male models in soft blue jeans and leather jackets.

And it was precisely as they began discussing models that they realised they'd hit a bit of a brick wall. The market fashion shows were really a bit of fun to help sell the clothes, using people's relatives and a few of the more eager wanna-bees from one of the local performing arts schools. Now they'd seen Jennie's plans and Cameron's atrium, they knew they needed professionals.

Alice scurried home and checked out Jennie's files again. Booking models wasn't a problem; Jennie had made a short-list of agencies. But as Alice picked up the phone to ring them on Wednesday morning, she froze mid-way through dialling the first number.

Just *where* was she going to hold a 'go-see' for these models? In the last two days her tiny rented bedroom had become a makeshift office, and was now mostly buried under bits of paper, hanging rails and boxes of clothes. Now when she fell into bed at night she had to scoop a whole load of mess off of her bed and dump it on her desk. The next morning she scooped it right up again and threw it back on the bed. She could hardly phone up the modelling agencies and ask them to send a steady stream of girls and boys to 27b Laburnham Terrace, so they could tramp up the narrow stairs and parade around in her boxroom. What sort of impression would *that* create?

She put her mobile on the only titchy free bit of space on her desk and stared at it. There was only one thing she could think of doing. Phoning Cameron. And she really, really didn't want to do that.

How could she face him again after the site meeting? Thank goodness she'd recovered a little when she'd seen the building and realised all the possibilities for the ball. She'd been able to block all the stupidity out for a while and talk sense. A shudder rippled through her as she remembered how she'd suddenly got all clumsy and wordless. She'd practically been drooling, for heaven's sake! No wonder she had no desire to repeat the humiliation.

Yes, okay, she knew they'd see each other again on the fourteenth—the night of the ball—but until then she'd hoped to keep things completely to e-mail. She'd already sent him a few lengthy updates, keeping him abreast of everything, pre-empting any more unexpected phone calls.

Why?

There was no point hiding from it. She'd got the hots for Cameron Hunter, and she'd got them bad. Which was a disastrous idea. She needed to be cool and professional to make a success of this project. Being so far out of her comfort zone, she was practically on a different planet.

She rested her elbows unevenly on top of some notebooks strewn across her desk and put her head in her hands. It was probably just some subconscious reaction to being recently dumped. Something to do with feeling on the shelf and unattractive. Just a subconscious thing.

And a physical thing. Definitely a physical thing.

Which was why she was aiming to keep being in the same room as him to a minimum. Perhaps then she'd have time to gather herself together. By the time the fashion show and the ball came around she'd be over it, and far too busy organising things on the night to even speak to him. And he'd be too busy mixing with the great and good on the guest list to want to talk to her. No, if she kept her distance, it would all work out fine.

But then there was the voice...

Log fires were so yesterday. Today's trend was *furnaces*. Every time he'd opened his mouth on their tour of the building she'd felt a fire lick the soles of her feet, and it had travelled up and up and up until her ears had burned and she'd been sure he'd notice the heightened colour in her cheeks.

Hence the e-mails. E-mails were good. E-mails didn't require her to stop listening to the actual words and just drift away on the warm, earthy sound of his voice...

Alice's eyes had slid shut and she snapped them open. *Stop it!* She picked up a bright yellow folder from her desk and fanned herself down with it. Was twenty-eight too young to be having hot flushes?

Now she thought about it there *was* a problem with the e-mails—the replies. When they arrived, and she read Cameron's sharp, concise verdict on her notes, she couldn't help picturing him standing on that balcony, standing so close to her that she'd been able to smell his clean, unfussy after-shave, close enough to see those warm flecks in his dark eyes. And that led to thinking about his rare, show-stopping smiles, and then her pulse would start to get all silly.

So, whichever way she looked at it, she was in big trouble. In which case she might as well just stop sitting here day-dreaming, pick up the phone and get it over and done with.

In a minute, anyway. She'd just look at her notes first.

She booted up her laptop. Her fingers were hovering over the keyboard when her phone rang. Her heart did a sickening lurch, as if it had tripped over its toes and gone tumbling down the stairs. She stared at it.

It was a number she didn't recognise.

Answer it, you fool!

What? Oh, right.

'Hello?'

'Hello, Alice.'

Whoomp. The furnace rushed into life.

'Hi, Cameron! I got the stuff you sent over.' Great. She'd been aiming to sound like a calm, professional woman and instead she'd got closer to Minnie Mouse.

'Were those files any help?' he asked, a slight tinge of desperation in his voice.

She spread the sheets out on her desk and frowned. 'I've only been able to leaf through so far, but Jennie seems to have a lot of the details covered. I suspect she may have booked musicians and caterers already, but I'll have to ring and check.'

Cameron made a noise that sounded suspiciously like a relieved sigh. 'Good. I'm glad it's not a complete disaster. Is there anything I can do to help?' he asked, and she took a deep breath and told herself to behave.

She explained about the models—the casting session, the lack of a suitable venue.

'We'll do it here,' he said, before she'd finished her last sentence. 'In fact I should have thought of the fact that you'd need space, an office...'

'But I've got—'

'You can have space here. There's a spare office in my suite, and you can use the meeting room for casting the models.'

Alice's face crumpled into a look of utter despair. 'Really, there's no need for an office. Just the meeting room would be fine. I can do the rest from—'

'It makes sense for you to be on hand. That way I can answer any queries immediately, approve things quickly, and you can stop flooding my inbox with charts and pages of notes.' It was only the faint edge of humour in that last comment that stopped her flinging the phone down on him.

What was it about this man that made it impossible to say no to him? It was like having an argument with a steamroller. One minute you were standing your ground, pleading your case, and the next you were flat on the floor, agreeing to everything he said and wondering what had hit you. If she was going to manage to work with him on this party—this *extravaganza*, as she was now beginning to think of it—she was going to have to start giving as good as she got, even if no one else seemed to do it.

She'd seen the way everyone at the building site had behaved around him. It was, *Yes, Mr Hunter... No, Mr Hunter*. Well, maybe not *no*. She hadn't actually heard anyone be brave enough to utter that word in his presence.

But she had an advantage his employees didn't have.

None of his staff had seen him playing ridiculous party games. That Christmas, after they'd escaped from the party, they'd eventually been discovered and told off for not joining in. His staff hadn't seen him trying to pass an orange to Aunty Barb with the thick foundation. It had been cringeworthy and hilarious all at the same time. Cameron had screwed up his face and desperately tried not to get smudged with make-up that was almost as bright as the fruit under his chin. He had failed miserably.

She'd just have to keep that image in mind every time he decided to get all high and mighty on her. Yep. That ought to do the trick.

* * *

Alice moved into a little office at Orion Solutions the following morning. It was a small space near the lifts, and nowhere as huge as some of the other rooms nearby, but that suited Alice just fine. She didn't want big and expansive. She wanted a little hole she could hide in until all this was over and done. Even though Cameron's office was on the same floor, her new office was as far away from his as it was possible to be without falling off the edge of the building. Hopefully that kind of geography would help her concentration.

Cameron had been as good as his word. He'd arranged for all of Alice's IT bookings for the next three weeks to be covered by a team of experts from Orion Solutions, and now she had a chance to live her dream and get a taste of what it was like to live and breathe vintage fashion without all that pesky computer stuff getting in her way.

At least, she'd be able to live and breathe vintage fashion once she got a few other annoying things off her mind. Yesterday evening she'd got an e-mail from Cameron's PA, letting her know he had arranged for them to have lunch together the following day to discuss preparations for the ball. There had only been his voicemail to talk to by the time she'd found the message. This morning she'd tried to ring him again, to cancel, but had been told he was out and would be meeting her at the restaurant. She should just make her way to the lobby at twelve-thirty, where somebody would meet her and let her know where to go.

She didn't even get a chance to explain that she'd rather *not* have lunch with the boss. The fact that someone might deviate from his instructions was obviously an unknown concept around here. So, while she should have been getting down to business—making calls, crossing things off her ever-expanding list—she spent most of her time worrying about seeing

Cameron in the flesh again, and whether her wardrobe today was going to be up to anywhere he was going to take her.

The chocolate trousers had had to make a reappearance. Alice discovered a burning need to go shopping for new work clothes. Her usual jeans and boots, more suited to crawling around on the floor looking at cables, just weren't going to cut it here at the rather upmarket Orion Solutions. All the men wore really nice suits, and the women looked sharp and smart, as if their feet didn't protest at all when they marched round the office all day in heels.

Alice's feet had protested at just being prised out of her comfy trainers and forced into a pair of low-heeled pumps.

Still, however scarily smart the Orion bunch seemed to be, they were all very friendly, and there seemed to be a lot of good-natured banter going on. Cameron's PA got her a coffee and chatted away so incessantly about him that Alice's eyes started to glaze over. It seemed she felt she'd found a kindred spirit.

At twelve-twenty-five Alice stepped into the lift and felt her stomach float and churn in a disturbing way as the doors closed and she started the downward journey. It seemed to go on for ever, and she was heartily relieved when they reached the lobby.

As soon as she stepped from the lift, a serious dark-suited young man who introduced himself as just 'Henderson' approached her, and indicated she should follow him. Alice trotted after him, wondering which sandwich bar they were headed for. But instead of leading her to a little café, with pictures of coffee cups on the windows, Henderson stopped in front of a long black limo and opened the door.

Alice just stared at him.

'We're eating in there?' she said, confusion written all over her face.

Henderson, bless him, didn't even crack a smile.

'No, madam. Mr Hunter would like you to join him up in town, and has asked me to drive you to the restaurant.'

Oh.

Work lunches to self-employed Alice meant a Thermos of soup or a ham salad bap and a packet of crisps. They obviously meant something totally different to Cameron Hunter.

Not wanting to seem even more gauche than she already had, she slid into the back seat of the limo, and didn't dare squeak another word until they arrived at their destination.

The drive out of Docklands into the West End seemed to fly past. Perhaps it was Alice's imagination, but the traffic seemed to melt away, deferring to the powerful, sleek black car. The other drivers probably imagined somebody famous or important was inside. That made her smile. It was like having a secret joke, seeing all the other traffic let them pass and knowing it was only ordinary old her on the other side of the tinted glass.

Henderson finally drew up outside an imposing hotel on the edge of Hyde Park, and before Alice could even thank him she was being ushered out of the car and into the foyer by a liveried doorman. From there she was escorted towards the restaurant, which was hidden behind a screen of glass shelves stacked with hundreds of bottles of wine. Even before she saw the restaurant she knew it was going to be somewhere scarily minimalist and trendy, and that she probably wouldn't recognise half the ingredients on the menu.

She smoothed down the hem of her soft heather-coloured polo neck as she followed the waiter to a table near the windows overlooking the park. There was no sign of Cameron, and she had no idea what time the table had been booked for, so she sat as still as she could and tried not to look too out of place.

A different waiter appeared and asked her if she'd like

some wine. She desperately wanted to say yes, but decided she needed a clear head and asked for water instead.

Where, oh, where was Cameron? Far from wanting to avoid meeting him, she was now desperate to see something—someone—who wasn't totally alien to her.

Two women in extremely expensive coats walked past her table.

'Did you see who was in the lobby?' the one in the camel coat asked the other one.

'No,' the other woman, who had bumped Alice with her massive shoulder bag as she passed, replied. 'Anyone we know?'

'Cameron Hunter,' Camel Coat muttered under her breath as she sat down at a table only a few feet away. 'I don't actually know him personally, but he used to go out with my sister.'

'Really? I think my cousin dated him once too.'

Alice's ears tingled. She didn't want to listen to this conversation, but she didn't have much choice. Apart from sticking her fingers in her ears and going *la-la-la*, there wasn't much she could do.

'Silly girl,' Large Shoulder Bag said with a sigh. 'I don't think there's a heart in London he hasn't broken. But she thought she was going to be the one to succeed where all the others had failed. Of course he ended it.'

Alice's urge to ram her index fingers in her ears was almost irresistible.

'Of course,' Camel Coat said sagely. 'He always does.'

'She should have known the score from the start—silly girl.'

CHAPTER FOUR

ALICE had her fingers ready, and was just about to lift them from under the tablecloth when she saw Cameron striding across the room. Something odd happened. An invisible ripple emanated from him, and everyone it touched straightened their spines, looked his way, then hurried on about their business. Even the two women in the coats stopped gossiping, thank goodness.

'Sorry I'm a little late,' he said, as he leaned over to kiss her cheek.

Alice burbled something noncommittal in reply. Stringing words into sentences was suddenly beyond her.

Immediately two—not one, but two—waiters snapped to attention at their table. Cameron ordered off-menu, and Alice let him pick for her too. She wasn't even sure she knew what 'ballotine of rabbit' or 'celeriac remoulade' were, anyway. And that was only from the list of starters!

But Cameron seemed completely at home with the waiters bobbing up and down, almost sprinting off to get him anything he desired, and Alice realised with astonishment that he was just as comfortable here as *she* would have been in that little café with the coffee cups on the window. This was *his* world.

Somehow she hadn't really believed all the millionaire software entrepreneur stuff up until now. Being slapped in the face with it was somewhat of a shock.

Thankfully, after they'd demolished their starters, they got on with discussing the ball, and she filled him in on the details of what Jennie had already booked and how the plans were progressing. Cameron seemed happy with everything she said, but somehow, Alice just couldn't seem to relax with him as she had the other day. It was as if she was seeing him with a completely fresh pair of eyes.

Was there even a hint of the sensitive, serious young man she'd known all those years ago? If there was, she was struggling hard to see it in him today. He was all quiet charm and confidence, understated power. There was something compelling and magnetic about him, and he drew every female eye in the busy restaurant, but Alice couldn't help feeling that she was sitting opposite a stranger.

Well, perhaps that was for the best. The past was the past, and she needed concentrate on the future—the next few weeks in particular. For that time period he would effectively be her boss. She was just another one of his paid minions.

He was all business during lunch, treating her as such. And that started to rankle with Alice. Even the divine food couldn't take her mind off her irritation. *She* was doing *him* a favour, actually, not the other way around. A smile now and then wouldn't go amiss. But he was so totally focussed on the project in hand it seemed he'd forgotten how to be…well, human.

Things didn't improve much when they headed back to the office. Alice returned to her own little room, and there she stayed, glued to the phone, frantically taking notes and generally filling the space with an ever-expanding mess that she wasn't quite sure Cameron would approve of.

Every time she thought of him, even when she remembered lunch with the cold, emotionless business tycoon, her whole body buzzed and she flushed hot and cold—just as she had that day at the building site. Time and distance didn't seem to dilute the effect he had on her, unfortunately. And neither did being in a slight strop with him.

She was starting to understand Jennie's multitude of doodles, because she'd caught herself in the act too. Nothing incriminating, like initials or love hearts, but it was the fact she was doodling at all that bothered her. She was supposed to be concentrating.

At the end of the day, when she'd made her last phone call and her to-do list had started to go all blurry, she headed for the lift. Just as the doors were about to close, a large hand sliced between them and pulled them open again. Alice didn't need to see the rest of the body to know who it was. All at once the blood in her veins started to hum.

Stop it! she told herself. *Stop it at once!*

Cameron merely nodded at her and stood silently beside her. And as they rode down in the lift together, preparing to go their separate ways to their separate homes, Alice held her breath and tried to anchor her stomach yet again.

Cameron turned to her.

'Thank you, Alice, for all you're doing.'

Alice struggled hard not to let her surprise at his words show on her face.

'I really enjoyed our lunch,' he added.

Had he? Had she been the only one feeling as if she was teetering on a tightrope the whole time, then?

And then he did something even more unexpected. He smiled at her. 'It reminded me of that Christmas party. Do you remember?'

He shuddered. And she knew as surely as she knew her own name that he was remembering Aunty Barb's orange foundation. The very same thought that had popped into her own mind.

The grin widened, suddenly taking years off him, changing his face from granite into something softer, warmer, and infinitely more alive, more appealing. Breathing suddenly became something less than automatic.

Oh, yes. She remembered.

With his unheralded smile Cameron had brought all those warm feelings rushing back. Alice couldn't help but smile back. Something clicked into place, and once again they were partners in crime.

Cameron knocked on the office door, but didn't wait for an answer before he pushed it open. Alice was on the phone. She glanced up at him, but almost too quickly her eyes flitted back to the large spiral-bound pad in front of her. As he stepped closer he saw that she wasn't taking notes, but filling in the detail of an elaborate doodle.

By the sounds of it she was talking to someone who hired out staging, and she was busy telling them, in her soft, understated voice, that what they were proposing to build for the fashion show catwalk just wasn't good enough, and could they please pass her on to someone who knew what they were talking about or she'd take her business elsewhere.

Alice might seem meek in person, but in the week she'd been based in the spare office on his floor he'd realised that underneath she was a woman who had very clear ideas about what she wanted and how she wanted it done. Once she'd set her mind on something, she wasn't easily shaken.

When she put the phone down she was almost smiling, and he surmised that she had indeed once again got her own way. Not by shouting or manipulating, but through quiet determination.

'You wanted to see me?'

She flushed an attractive shade of pale pink. A shade that matched the simple embroidered blouse she was wearing. While other women in the office either power-dressed or wore bland outfits he hardly even noticed, Alice always wore something that caught his attention. Not that what she wore wasn't suitable for the office—just that somehow he stopped and looked. Perhaps it was the vintage fashion angle. If so, that boded well for the ball and the fashion show. It certainly would be memorable if every outfit had this effect on every guest.

Alice looked apologetic. 'Oh… no. I mean—I didn't mean you had to drop what you were doing. It could have waited.'

Yes, it could have. He had calls to make, reports to read, marketing meetings to attend. But somehow wandering into Alice's temporary office had seemed much more appealing.

The room had been bare less than a week ago, only a desk and a dead pot plant occupying the space. Now there were clothing rails, sketches stuck haphazardly to the walls, and two dilapidated mannequins staring at him, rather as if they were keeping guard. The one on the right only had one good eye, and the effect of her bright green stare was rather unnerving. He moved his gaze away from the bald-headed figure to look back at Alice.

'Here I am,' he said. 'Ready to do your bidding.'

She seemed to find that funny, because her eyes shone and she pressed her lips together, squashing a smile away. He couldn't help smiling back. Not his nice-to-do-business-with-you smile, but a real one—a lazy one that gently lifted the corners of his mouth. That seemed to have an odd effect on Alice, because she stopped being all cheeky and started tidying things on her desk, squaring her notepad, dropping paperclips in a pot.

He couldn't make this woman out.

Sometimes she reminded him of the quiet, shy girl he'd known years ago. Sometimes she was a confident, strong-minded professional. But then she'd get all absent-minded and start knocking things over, spoiling the polished picture. It didn't matter, though, that he couldn't solve the riddle that was Alice. He just enjoyed watching her slip from one persona to another, wondering what she would do next.

And in that respect their relationship seemed to be a two-way street. It was refreshing to be in the company of someone who didn't label him as just one thing—a software tycoon, a hard-nosed businessman. Or a meal ticket.

She stood up and walked round to the front of the desk, leaned back against it. 'We need to find you something to wear for the party,' she said, looking him up and down.

Now, hang on a minute. There was no *way* he was wearing second-hand clothes to the biggest event of his career. Not when he'd invited specific people just so he could rub their noses in his success. He'd been there, done that, worn the T-shirt— literally—and he'd promised himself he'd never do it again.

He gave her a steely look and shook his head. Alice didn't bat an eyelid. Most of his employees would have bowed and backed out of the room if they'd been on the receiving end of that look.

'Everyone else on your senior management team has agreed to wear something vintage—even if it's only a waist-coat or a hat.'

'I am *not* wearing a hat.'

The little smile was back. 'All right. Don't get your knickers in a twist.' She rolled her eyes and walked over to the clothing rails, where she started moving things around. Beneath the sound of scraping hangers he could have sworn he'd heard her mutter something along the lines of, 'Obviously it's a crown or nothing, then.'

A few moments later she held up an ensemble. 'Everyone else has agreed to be a little adventurous. How about this?'

Jeans and a leather jacket? She had to be joking.

'Try it on,' she said. 'We put a screen in the corner so the models could get changed for the casting session the other day.'

She thrust the hanger at his chest and let go, and he didn't have much choice but to grab onto it to stop it all landing in a heap at his feet. See? Quiet determination. Alice liked having her own way just as much as he did.

Leather jackets were so not him. He'd never been a rebel—had always had a clear vision of where he wanted to go in life. Messing around hadn't ever been on the timetable. But the faded denim was soft between his fingers, and the smell of the leather made him think of motorbikes and open roads.

'Okay,' he mumbled. 'I'll try it on. But I'm telling you this: I'm *not* wearing it to the party.' His staff would all fall about laughing.

He marched behind the screen and started to undress, wondering as he did so just how he'd ended up stripping down to his boxers in the middle of a Thursday afternoon. He was taller than the screen, and as he pulled on the clothes Alice had given him he kept catching glimpses of her as she shuffled papers on her desk and generally ignored him. He couldn't remember the last time a woman had been so clearly unaffected by the thought of him being semi-naked in the same room as her. It was probably good for his ego. It didn't mean he liked it, though.

Finally he was done. The jeans were a perfect fit—felt as

if he'd owned them for years, had *lived* in them. The white T-shirt was brand-new, thankfully. It was crisp and clean and still had the sales tag attached. As he rounded the screen he shoved his arms into the leather jacket and pulled it over his shoulders.

Alice seemed to be doing that silent, unimpressed-but-rooted-to-the-spot thing she did, but her eyes were round and she was staring at him.

'Happy?' he said, in a voice that was a tad gruffer than he'd intended it to be.

Alice just nodded.

'Very,' she whispered, when she finally got her voice. 'You've got it… Um…it's caught…'

She walked over to him, not looking him in the eye, and sorted out the lapel of the jacket, which had somehow got tucked under itself, smoothing it into place. He stared at her small, long-fingered hand as it came to rest on his chest, on the white T-shirt.

'You're right,' she said, and then gave a little cough to clear her throat. 'It looks…g-good…but it's not right for the party.'

'Uh-huh,' he heard himself say. He'd been staring at her cheekbones and had got distracted by the translucent quality of her skin. Like most redheads she was pale—almost white—but she seemed to glow. How did she do that? He ran his tongue across his dry bottom lip, all at once overtaken by the urge to find out what a *glow* like that might taste like.

'No,' she said.

No to what? To glowing? To *tasting*…?

'I'll find you something else.'

And before he'd had a chance to say James Dean she'd darted away and hidden herself between the racks of clothes.

Nothing else worked. Cameron tried not to think about who might have been the last person to wear each of the five suits he tried on, tried not to think about mothballs and funerals and caskets. Just as well that none of them fitted. Either the trouser legs flapped above his ankles or the shoulders were way too tight.

'I happen to have some really nice suits of my own,' he yelled over the top of the screen as he finally clambered back into his own clothes. 'The one I was intending to wear—to *my* party, remember?—is being made for me by a man on Savile Row.'

She looked impressed when he mentioned the name, clearly knowing that the man in question never needed to advertise and that being admitted into the inner sanctum of his fitting rooms was rather like gaining entry to an exclusive gentlemen's club.

'Sizing with vintage clothes is often a problem for someone as tall and… Well, with all those…with all that—with your physique,' she finished in a hurry. 'We could search for months and not find anything suitable. A few *distinctive* vintage accessories may be the way to go. I'll see what I can find.'

He shrugged his suit jacket back on and straightened his tie. 'In other words, the last forty-five minutes were a complete waste of time?'

She pulled an apologetic face.

'My time is valuable,' he said, trying not to smile. 'I should charge you.'

Suddenly she looked extremely serious and thoughtful. 'It'd be worth every penny,' she said, glancing at the leather jacket and jeans hanging innocently on the other side of the room, a decidedly naughty twinkle in her eye.

Wait a minute. Was Alice…*flirting* with him? In a totally *Alice* way, of course. She'd just hinted at it with that look, done something almost undetectable with her voice. It was all so subtle he started to doubt it had been there in the first place.

When he looked again she was hanging the last of the suits up, all brisk efficiency, and he decided he must have imagined it after all.

His forehead crinkled into a slight frown.

The thought he might have imagined it disappointed him, and the realisation he was disappointed surprised him. Did he *want* Alice to flirt with him? She was just a kid he'd once been kind to at a Christmas party a very, very long time ago. As she walked back to her desk she did the hair-behind-the-ear gesture. The gentle, unselfconsciously feminine movement made his stomach knot, even though she wasn't paying him the slightest bit of attention. All at once surprise gave way to irritation. Another thing he didn't like. This feeling of being at a disadvantage, of not being the one to hold all the cards.

'Am I dismissed, then?' he asked, as she tucked herself behind the desk and got back to work.

She looked up at him, bit her lip and released it slowly, emphasising its fullness. Somehow that just made him crosser.

'Yes.' The cool, restrained tone was back, but there was something—an undercurrent—that made him eye her suspiciously. 'I've finished dressing you up. You can go now.'

Well, he didn't know how to respond to that. Nobody ever dismissed him. He didn't like that much, either.

'Fine. I will, then.'

And he crashed out of the door and down the hallway without looking back.

Alice stared after him. Was she going crazy? She certainly seemed to be behaving strangely today. She swung round on her chair and looked out of the window. First of all she'd made Cameron get dressed up in an outfit she'd known he would never consent to wear to the party—just on a whim.

She sighed. It had been *so* worth it.

And just now, only a few seconds ago, had she actually been *flirting*?

Well, it hadn't done her much good, had it? He'd gone all prickly and she'd just got worse, goading a reaction out of him. Well done, Alice. You just sent Cameron Hunter packing when he's the key to your whole future. Very professional. But it was just... Well, when Cameron pushed, she had the stupidest urge to push back twice as hard.

What was wrong with her? She was doormat girl—voted by everyone she knew as most likely to just lie down and take rubbish from the men in her life—and she'd decided to lock horns with Cameron Hunter? Great time to grow a backbone, Alice.

Aw, shut up. You've always had a spine and you know it. You just chose to put it out to pasture because it suited your plan of being the perfect low-stress girlfriend no man could resist.

And look how well *that* had turned out. Yet another well-thought-out plan.

She let out a deep breath and rubbed her eyes. It must be the long hours, being flung into the deep end of her new career—and Jennie's—without really knowing what she was doing.

A sudden blush crept up her cheeks.

Keeping her tongue under control hadn't been the only problem, had it? Her hands seemed to have developed a will of their own too. But that white T-shirt had smelled of warm, clean man and had looked all soft and fresh and...touchable. She'd been feeling the heat of his chest beneath her palm before she'd even registered a decision to put it there.

This was bad. The party and the fashion show were in another nine days, and then she'd be back in the real world—not stuck up here in this impossibly high tower where the altitude must be getting to her brain cells. She couldn't let this ill-timed crush grow any further.

I mean, get real, Alice. It's all just a fairy tale, a daydream. He dates the likes of socialites and supermodels. If you can't hold on to the likes of geeky Paul, how in hell have you got a chance of keeping a man like Cameron Hunter interested?

Two hours later, Alice was knocking on Coreen's door. Coreen answered, resplendent in an embroidered black silk kimono and a bright green face pack. Alice pushed past her, marched into the kitchen, grabbed two wine glasses out of the cupboard and started pouring cheap Cabernet from the screwtop bottle she'd brought with her.

Coreen skidded into the kitchen behind her. 'Whoa!' she said, her eyes widening as Alice filled the oversized glasses nearly to the brim. Her voice sounded funny, escaping through clenched teeth as she tried not to crack her face mask. 'What happened?'

Alice picked the glasses up and handed one to Coreen. Her hand was shaking and she sloshed wine all over her fingers. Shaking her head, she slammed the glass down, spilling more.

'Me. *I* happened. I've had an epiphany! I'm the anti-girlfriend.'

Coreen's face mask crumbled, and large chunks rained down on her kimono. She shook her head. 'This is all about Paul, isn't it?' she said. 'You're going through the five stages of grief…I thought you were in denial; now you've obviously moved on to anger.' She stared at Alice. 'What happened to bargaining? You should be bargaining now.'

Alice took another swig of wine and held it in her mouth for a second before swallowing it. She nodded at the bottle and headed out of the kitchen. 'How's this for bargaining? You keep the red stuff coming and I'll tell you all about it!'

Coreen had no choice but to follow her into the sitting

room, where Alice not so much sat down as crumpled onto the couch.

'Now, what's all this about you being an anti-girlfriend? Is it like being an anti-hero? I'm not sure I quite get it.'

'More like being an antidote,' Alice said gloomily. 'And not in a good way.' She sank back into the sofa and stared into space. 'I know what Paul meant when he said I was "a relief" now. Men *love* those girly girls.' She narrowed her eyes and looked at Coreen. 'Girls like you. Pretty girls, who run them a merry dance and keep them on their toes. Girls who torture them and treat 'em mean to keep 'em keen. But after a while either she gets tired of him not being up to scratch, or he gets tired of all the game-playing and one of them ends it. And that's when the guys come looking for me—the perfect antidote to a demanding diva.'

'That's good news, surely?' Coreen said. She thought a while, then pouted. 'Not for girls like me, of course. But for girls like you it is.' She grinned, destroying the rest of the face pack completely, and held her hand up for a high five.

'What do all my exes have in common?' Alice asked in a wistful voice.

'Erm…bad hair?'

Alice shook her head, and kept on staring at the paisley curtains.

'Anoraks?' Coreen ventured, and got a scowl for her efforts.

'I figured it out on the way over here.'

'Figured *what* out?'

'All of them said how lovely I was—how *easy* I was to be around. Easy to dump when something better turned up, more like it.' Alice turned to look at her. 'I am—and will only ever be—a *transition* girlfriend.'

'I thought you said you were an antidote…'

'They all say they are fed up with the high-maintenance women in their lives, but they all eventually find a new siren to trot around after—or, in Paul's case, trot back to.' Her face fell. 'I'm just a…a…*stopgap* until that happens!'

Coreen flung her arms round Alice and squeezed. 'You are so much more than a stopgap!'

'Then why don't the guys I go out with get that?' she wailed. 'Why am I always the one they go out with just *before* they find the love of their lives? Why can't somebody think *I'm* the most wonderful thing to happen to them for a change?'

Coreen hugged her tighter. 'You want the truth?'

Alice nodded. If her friend had some advice on how she should keep men interested, she might as well hear it. She was tired of being discarded like an old shoe.

'I think that until *you* believe you're more than a stopgap, you're going to keep attracting men like Paul. He was too much of an idiot to see what he had.' Coreen swivelled to face her. 'Where's all this coming from anyway? I don't think this is all about Pathetic Paul after all.'

Alice avoided her gaze. 'Nonsense. Of course it is. I've been so busy recently, when have I had time to meet any other men?'

A naughty smile quirked Coreen's lips. 'There *is* one rather yummy specimen you've come into contact with on a daily basis recently.' She paused and looked a little sheepish. 'I Googled him, you know.'

'Who?' Alice said, fearing she already knew the answer.

'Mr Orion Solutions, of course.' Her eyes brightened. 'Did you know he went out with—?' She took one look at Alice's face and closed her mouth. 'Never mind…'

Alice sighed. 'Yes, I know he went out with Sierra Collins last year. Suddenly I keep seeing her face everywhere. On bus shelters, batting her eyelashes at me…in my bathtime magazine, showing off her perfect bikini body…I think I hate her.'

Coreen sighed too, and flumped back onto the sofa next to Alice. 'She's a supermodel. What's not to hate?'

They sat in silence for a few minutes.

'You like him, don't you?' Coreen finally said, so quietly it was almost a whisper.

'I do *not*!' Alice said with venom, and then buried her face in a cushion. Coreen tapped her on the shoulder, and Alice looked up. 'Oh, Corrie…I really do. I really do like him. A lot. It's like a bad joke, really.'

A soppy smile spread across Coreen's face. 'Aww, I can see it now—childhood sweethearts, and then he whisks you off your feet and takes you away from all this…'

Alice burst out laughing. 'I hardly think so! He was lovely back then, you know. Sensitive, thoughtful, kind…I'm sure he's still that way underneath, but he's changed, Corrie. He's used to the finest things in life, to having the best of everything. Somehow he's harder, pushier. It wouldn't be a good idea to get involved with him. It really wouldn't.'

'Not even a teensy bit?' Coreen replied, her incorrigible smile back on her face.

Alice laughed again, but this time it was more with gallows humour than hysteria. She walked over to Coreen's stack of fashion magazines and flicked through one, then another. Finally she found what she was looking for. She folded the magazine back on itself and held the picture up next to her face.

On one side the glossy picture of Sierra Collins—flawless skin, sparkling blue eyes, a cleavage…

On the other, plain old Alice Morton. So used to being 'one of the lads' she was almost androgynous, with her face flushed pink and a figure like an ironing board.

Coreen looked at both Alice and the magazine picture, her eyes sombre.

'I rest my case,' said Alice, and threw herself back down on the sofa.

Coreen silently handed her back her glass of wine, patting her on the hand.

'And you know why?' Alice went on. 'I learned my lessons from *Anne of Green Gables*.'

Coreen blinked. 'What on earth are you talking about?'

Alice hugged her wine glass to her chest and let it warm her fingers as she gazed off into the distance. 'Anne went searching everywhere to find her Mr Right—looking for dashing strangers, full of adventure—and where did she find him?'

Coreen opened her mouth, but Alice didn't give her the chance to provide her with a smart answer.

'She found him right underneath her nose! Gilbert!'

A blank look crossed Coreen's face.

'The boy next door that she'd always been in love with but never realised until it was almost too late. Well, I'm not going to be that stupid. There are plenty of ordinary, lovely guys right under our noses—I just have to find which one's mine.'

Coreen snorted. 'Well, you go on looking under rocks, or whatever, but you can count me out.' Then she went very still. 'Anne of Green Gables? Wasn't she the one who said she'd die if she didn't get a pair of puff sleeves?'

Alice bit her lip and nodded.

Coreen took a large slurp of wine. 'Now, *there's* a sentiment I can agree with,' she said, as she waved her glass at Alice.

CHAPTER FIVE

A WEEK later Alice was starting to think that nothing else existed but the inside of Cameron's spare office and this blasted *extravaganza* she was planning. There had never been anything else. There never would be anything else. Eternity would be full of to-do lists, phone calls and an inbox that clogged up faster than she could unclog it. She ought to keep a plunger under her desk for the very purpose.

The ball to celebrate the opening of Cameron's new building was in two days, and she was fantasising about slipping into a coma when it was all over and done with.

Thankfully, Jennie was obviously marvellous at her job, and it hadn't been as hard as she'd expected to pick up the reins; it had just made life very, very busy. All of Jennie's suppliers and contacts had been wonderful when she'd phoned them and explained that Jennie was on her honeymoon and she was the new girl filling in. But with a job this size it was inevitable that there would be a multitude of last-minute hitches. It was eating up all her time.

And somehow, at some point in the next forty-eight hours, she had to find herself a dress to wear.

She pushed her swivel chair away from the desk and let it

slide backwards. Her shoulders were all bunched up, and she rolled them a couple of times in an attempt to release them. They complained loudly. There was a headrest on her chair, and she let her head fall against it...

'No napping on the job, Morton!'

Alice easily resisted the urge to jump to attention, and lifted one eyelid. 'Hi, Coreen. What are you doing here? Shouldn't you be at the market?'

Coreen shook her head. 'Dawn looked after the stall for me today—and besides, the market closed an hour and a half ago.'

Already? Now the evenings were drawing in, and it was dark by five, it was easy to lose track of time. She raised her arms above her head and stretched.

Coreen started bouncing on her rather spectacular platforms. 'Anyway, I have something utterly *fabulous* to show you!'

Alice eyed the garment carrier Coreen was clutching with interest.

'I've found *your* dress.'

'*My* dress?'

Coreen's grin was a little scary as she unzipped the bag and pulled out the most amazing—

Alice was dumbstruck. In a flash, she was out of her chair and across the room.

'That can't be mine,' she said, her hands over her mouth. 'It's too... It's too...'

'Nonsense. It's nothing of the sort. It's fabulous.'

Of course it was fabulous. It was a gorgeous deep emerald satin—a floor-length bias-cut evening gown. The most beautiful thing she'd ever seen.

But it would look stupid on her. What about her hair? She opened her mouth to say so.

'Na-huh!' Coreen held up a finger and wagged it at her.

'Don't you *dare* say it. This is a genuine Elsa Schiaparelli and it's going to look stunning on you—I have a gut instinct about these things and you know it.'

Alice had to reach out and touch the fabric, feel its glossy weight, run the thick satin between her fingertips.

'Where did you get this?' she whispered.

Coreen's smile buckled a little. 'At an auction.'

'An auction!' They *never* bought clothes at specialist auctions. The clothes there were normally designer labels, exceptional quality, and way out of their price range. They'd never make back what they spent on clothes like that on a poky little market stall. 'How much did it cost?'

'I paid a quarter of what it's worth,' Coreen said. 'If you're worried about the money, you don't have to keep it. We can auction it off at the party. Along with all the rest…'

Alice's eyelid began to twitch, and she looked at Coreen.

'What exactly do you mean by "the rest"?'

Something was different. Cameron had just been heading for the lifts, at the end of a long day, but halfway down the corridor he stopped. He didn't know what it was, but something was definitely…not *wrong*, but different. He just had to work out what it was.

There was an extra light on somewhere. And then he noticed a fuzzy yellow slash on the carpet at the far end of the hall, emanating from the office he'd given Alice.

He stood in the semi-dark, looking at it.

He'd tried not to go into that office too much in the last week, but somehow he kept finding himself in there, even though he had plenty of reasons to be busy—plenty of reasons to keep him tied up for hours. With his normal workload, plus all the extra stuff involved with moving premises in the next few weeks, he'd been up at the crack of dawn and sliding into bed in the small hours of the morning. Perhaps it was tiredness, then. Maybe that explained the strange tug he felt towards that particular room.

And it didn't just stop at the doorway. Once he was inside, other strange things happened.

He'd spent years crafting a persona to fit his ambitions, and even more years shaping himself to make it all real, but when he was in Alice's office he found he forgot to be himself. He did uncharacteristic things—laughing, teasing, even talking about things that weren't business related. And the atmosphere in there heightened his senses. He noticed little things he was sure he normally missed: the delicate curve of an ear, a faint scent of floral perfume, the way her fingers curled around her pencil. Yes, something odd was definitely going on in that room. He made a mental note to get the air-conditioning checked out.

While he was standing in the half-light of the corridor, a noise came from the direction of Alice's office. It was a shout of frustration, immediately followed by the sound of rustling paper, as if a folder had been hurled across the room. Suddenly he was running, and when he rounded the office door loose leaf pages were still fluttering towards the floor.

Alice was sitting at the desk, her head in her hands, muttering to herself.

'Alice? Is everything okay?'

She started, and a further pile of papers ended up on the floor as she jumped up and jogged them with her elbow. 'Sorry…I'm having a bit of a tantrum.'

He shook his head. Alice didn't do tantrums. She did calm and collected—just like him.

'Do you need me to fetch someone?'

She looked thoughtful for a moment, then leaned forward over the desk. 'Know any hit men?' She seemed to droop. 'The only way to cope at times like this is to descend into humour. Very dark humour, it seems.'

'Problems?'

She nodded. 'Coreen got a little carried away today. You remember Coreen, don't you?'

How could he forget? When she visited Alice at the office here she looked him up and down as if he were a prime piece of beef. He had half an idea she'd once been on the verge of chasing him down the corridor and pinning him to his desk. Yes, he remembered Coreen. She was definitely a young lady with the capability to get more than a little carried away.

He walked over to the desk and perched on the edge. Alice looked up at him. She was wearing a soft cream cardigan with woolly embroidery and little pearls dotted all over it. Was it cashmere? Must be. That would explain his urge to reach out and touch it—touch her. His fingers tingled with the need to do just that.

'Coreen went to a vintage clothing auction today, because she wanted to pick up a couple of dresses for the finale of the fashion show. She lucked out. A rather famous heiress had recently died, after reaching the grand old age of ninety-two, and all her wardrobe was up for sale.'

'Surely that's a good thing?'

Alice twirled a pencil on the desk, and Cameron's eyes followed the motion of her fingers.

'It would have been if she'd stuck at one or two of the smaller pieces. But she went a little loco and bought the lot.' She looked up at him and placed a reassuring hand on his arm—before whipping it away again. 'Don't worry. It won't affect the party or the fashion show.'

He looked at her hand, now back on the edge of the desk. 'It sounds like there's more to it than that.' He made a point of peering at the collection of papers littered all over the office floor.

She sighed. 'We'd been saving. For our own shop. Coreen's dipped into our start-up fund and almost wiped it out. If we don't get back what we paid for them... Well, let's just say we're taking a bit of a risk.'

She met his gaze, and he felt an odd little surge of something deep inside. They weren't the most stunning eyes he'd ever seen—not if you only counted shape and structure—but they were possibly the most unusual. They had...depth.

Tonight they'd lost some of their sparkle. Tonight they looked weary.

She must be exhausted.

Exhausted working for *him*, bailing him out of the hole Jennie had left for him. And he hadn't heard a murmur of complaint until her outburst this evening—and even that wasn't directed at him. He should have realised, done more... But he'd been too busy enjoying her company to think about making her go home earlier or insisting she take a day off. *You're selfish, Cameron.*

He stood in front of her and held out a hand. 'Come on.'

She raised her eyebrows and looked at him suspiciously. 'I was kidding about the hit man thing. You know that, don't you?'

There it was. The room was working its magic. He realised he was smiling.

'I know,' he said softly.

She blinked and looked away. But her pale fingers met his and she slid her hand into his waiting palm.

Alice felt like a firework inside—a firework whose fuse had been lit and which was jittering, waiting, until it fizzed and then shot into the sky. Cameron had led her back to his office and motioned for her to sit on the ridiculously long leather sofa while he headed for the phone. But she didn't seem to be feeling very obedient this evening, and she ignored the deep cushions in favour of the vast window that spanned the entire width of Cameron's office.

Her little office had a fantastic view too, but it was just round the corner of the building, and partially blocked by another skyscraper. Cameron's view was unobstructed and faced towards the heart of the city. They were so high up, and the window so clean, it was kind of like being suspended in mid-air, far away from the blinking lights, the red steaks of tail lights, the flashing aircraft. It was a beautiful view—the best—but she couldn't help feeling it was a little lonely up here too.

He was behind her. Suddenly she just knew it. The soft hair behind her ears lifted.

'It's beautiful,' she said. The silence needed to be broken, and stating the obvious was as good a way as any.

'Yes.' His voice was low and slightly husky.

She closed her eyes and placed a palm on the glass. *Think of Aunty Barb and oranges...*

Control yourself, Alice. It's just a little crush. It'll pass. And you know why? Just open your eyes, look at where you are, and you'll remember that you're from different worlds. You're a mere mortal, while he's...he's...Cameron Hunter.

She made herself do just that. But instead of seeing the lights, the dark indigo clouds edged with silver, all she could see was Cameron's reflection—and he was watching her.

Time skipped. She caught her breath and held it.

No, she must be mistaken. He wouldn't—*couldn't*—be looking at her that way. It must be a trick of the light as it bounced off this tinted glass.

Maybe it had been only wishful thinking, because when she turned around to look at him he was the same old Cameron, his eyes unreadable, almost blank.

'You must be hungry,' he said, and everything she'd been feeling crashed back down to earth. Practicalities. Reality. Yes, let's talk about those things for a while. Perhaps they'd get these daft notions out of her head.

'I've ordered a takeaway,' he added, still staring at her. 'I don't think either of us is in the mood for polite chit-chat in a restaurant.'

She began to protest, but he held up a hand.

'It's the least I can do to say thank you. You've worked your socks off to get me out of a nasty jam.'

Alice should have known that Cameron's definition of a takeaway would be vastly different from her own. No greasy paper-wrapped parcels for Mr Cameron Hunter—oh, no. Their meal was delivered from one of the local 'happening' restaurants. When the bags had been handed over and the delivery driver tipped—very generously, by the looks of it— Cameron walked to his desk and began moving stuff aside.

'What are you doing?' she asked.

Cameron paused, looking puzzled. 'Clearing a space. I always eat at my desk. You can have my chair, and I can pull up—'

Alice shook her head, effectively cutting him off. 'You can't eat takeaway sitting at your desk—like you're pretending you're at a fancy restaurant.'

'But this *is* restaurant food.'

Alice walked to a space in the centre of the vast royal-blue carpet, dropped onto her bottom and crossed her legs. 'To really appreciate the flavours and textures of a takeaway you have to picnic. Honestly, it makes the food taste better.'

Cameron looked as if he was going to choke. 'You want me to eat my dinner off the *floor*?'

'No.' She made a quick gesture with her hand, indicating that he should just stop making a fuss and pass the food over. She was starving, for goodness' sake! 'I'm saying we should *sit* on the floor and eat off the plates they've provided.'

For the first time since she'd known him she witnessed Cameron in a state of bemusement. It was quite funny, actually. He obediently picked up the bags of food, crossed the room, and awkwardly lowered himself down so he was sitting beside her. His trouser legs had ridden up and she could see his socks. Somehow that made him seem more human, less dangerous.

So from now on, Alice, if you get thoughts above your station, you can think about Aunty Barb, bruised oranges and *socks*. Okay?

The food was gorgeous, and Alice discovered she wasn't just starving, she was ravenous. As they made a dent in the multitude of cartons Cameron had ordered, he began to lose some of the hard angles from his posture, began to relax, and they chatted about work and the plans for the ball before changing the subject to books they'd read but hated. And from there they moved onto family news. Alice realised she knew a lot about Jennie, but knew hardly anything about Cameron. Since he seemed as laid back as she'd ever seen him, she decided to satisfy her curiosity.

'So, how old were you when your mum married Jennie's dad?'

There was a slight pause before he answered, as if she'd caught him off guard and he was regrouping.

'Seventeen.'

Cameron spent an inordinate amount of time staring at his food.

Twin urges, equal in force, took hold of her. Half of her wanted to heed the 'keep out' warnings he was radiating—his stiff posture, the failure to meet her eyes. He wanted her to leave this subject well alone, which was odd, because his and Jennie's blended family seemed so happy. The other half of her wanted to say *What the hell* to the warning signs and poke around a bit.

Tonight was a night for strange alliances—her and Cameron, five-star food and a carpet picnic—and Alice embraced the part of herself she'd usually tell to shut up.

'And before that? You never mention your own father.'

The atmosphere around them thickened. Cameron looked at her. 'Okay, technically the man had a minor part to play in my existence—' he looked vaguely disgusted at the thought '—but to earn the title of "father" one needs to care about one's offspring. To me, that man is nothing but an unfortunate biological connection.'

She wanted to reach for his hand, but sensed he'd shrug it off, was feeling too raw to let anyone touch him. She'd hit a nerve. A big one. Her instincts had been right. Despite his reluctance, Cameron needed to talk about this. It was burning a hole deep inside of him.

She kept her next question simple. 'When did he leave?'

He stared blankly at the wall. 'Fifteen days before my twelfth birthday.'

Tiny pieces of expressions he was trying desperately to hide flitted across his face. She guessed he was watching the memories play out in his mind. Maybe if she gave him space, just sat back and waited, he'd open up and—

'He was tired of us.'

Cameron blinked. Almost as if he was surprised at his own outburst. She held her breath, waiting to see if the rest would come.

He started off quietly, slowly, and then the words began to flow. 'He didn't like the domestic routine, our ordinary lives. Thought he was too good for it—that he deserved better.' He tore his gaze from the blank patch of wall and looked her in the eye. 'My mother and I weren't enough for him, so he jacked it all in to move to the Costa Brava with a barmaid from the local pub. Haven't seen him since.'

Alice inhaled. That was possibly the longest speech about personal matters she'd ever heard Cameron make.

'I'm so sorry,' she said, feeling completely inadequate to do or say anything to make it all better.

He shrugged. The mask was back.

'I don't care about knowing him. I haven't lost anything with his departure. What made me cross was the mess he left my mother in. My father had been a head teacher, on a very good salary, and suddenly all that was gone. Struggling along as a one-parent family was hard for her. We had to sell the house... She went from being a housewife to working two jobs just to keep food on the table and a roof over our heads.'

Alice pushed a container of spiced rice in his direction, trying to keep things as light and normal as possible, afraid she would spook him if she showed any emotion whatsoever.

'I didn't know that,' she said. 'I knew you went to St Michael's College, so I just…assumed.'

The exclusive boys' school just outside Greenwich had a stellar reputation and even higher fees. She'd never have guessed Cameron and his mother had had it so hard before she'd remarried.

He dug his fork into his rice and left it there. 'Scholarship. I was in my second term when Dad left and the money dried up, but I took the test and they let me stay on.'

'You must have been really grateful for that.'

Cameron let out a dry laugh. 'When I think of my school days, *grateful* is not the word that comes to mind—believe me.'

He stood up and walked to the window, leaving his half-eaten meal behind. Alice got the impression that he'd reached his limit, and she decided to turn the conversation in another direction and hopefully cheer him up in the meantime. She uncurled herself and got up.

'I'll just be a second,' she said, and raced down the hallway to her little office. When she returned, Cameron was still staring out of the window, but she doubted he was actually noticing anything.

Here goes.

'You know you said you'd wear something vintage to the party?'

He looked at her over his shoulder. 'Nice try, but I don't think I actually agreed to anything.'

Technically, he was right. But she wasn't going to let that stop her. 'But you didn't disagree—so by default you agreed.'

A sudden laugh burst from him, surprising both of them.

'You're a very persistent woman, Alice.'

She gave him a sheepish smile. 'Sorry.'

'Don't be,' he said as he walked towards her. 'I like it.'

In an effort to hide the horrible giddiness that had just overcome her, she pulled out the first of the items in the bag she'd had stashed under her desk for a few days, opened the little box, and held it out for him to see.

'Cufflinks?'

His eyebrows rose but he didn't lose his smile, which had to be a good sign. Alice reminded herself to breathe out.

'They're very…unusual,' he said.

The cufflinks were a simple Art Deco octagon—she had

passed over many more intricate designs, knowing Cameron would prefer something simple, understated and elegant.

He picked one of the cufflinks out of its cushion with a thumb and forefinger. 'What's the stone in the centre?'

She swallowed. 'Tiger's eye.'

They reminded me of you. But I can't tell you that.

Another gift was in the bag, and she made a show of rummaging for it to hide the blush that was about to give her away. When she looked up again, he was removing the cufflinks from his midnight-blue shirt cuffs and placing them on the edge of the desk, where they rolled to and fro slightly. Platinum, no doubt. With diamonds.

See, Alice? *There's* your proof of why you can say nothing, why you should rob this silly crush of oxygen until it suffocates. You give him old silver and semi-precious stones when he has the ability to buy the most exquisite jewellery from the world's top designers. Why would he want anything you have to give him?

She almost pushed her second gift back into the bag, suddenly horribly afraid it would miss the mark, like a prank gone wrong, but Cameron was busy admiring his new cufflinks. He stopped to look at her. 'I like them. They're diff…' He paused, and then a small smile curved his lips. 'They're *distinctive.'*

She couldn't help but smile softly back at him.

'If you think *they're* different, wait till you see what I've got in here.' And she shoved the bag towards him and took a swift step back once it was in his grasp.

Cameron took a moment to study the small black gift bag with gold ribbons for handles. *Coreen's Closet* was stamped over the front, in blocky letters that reminded him of old movie posters. He gathered up his courage and peeked into the bag.

'It's a tie,' he said, feeling relief wash through him. And for something old, once discarded, it was a rather nice tie—deep green silk, so dark it was very nearly black. The perfect match for the charcoal suit he'd be wearing. He looked up at Alice without bothering to hide his surprise.

'Thank you,' he said. 'I'll make sure I return these in good condition after the party.'

Alice flushed a deep pink—at least that was the way it seemed in the subdued light from his desk lamp. She shook her head. 'They're a gift.'

Cameron didn't know what to say—he didn't do *gushing*. He'd had many gifts from women in the last few years, much more expensive than this, but he knew that he could probably search the world over and never find duplicates of these things. And no one had ever given him something that summed him up in a way he couldn't even verbalise. Alice *knew* him. That should have worried him, had him running for the fire escape, but it didn't. Instead he just felt something akin to relief—as if he could breathe out for once.

'So you'll wear them for the party?'

Her question caught him by surprise. Did she honestly think he'd be that rude? He'd have worn them even if he'd hated them, but as it was he was warming up to the idea of joining in with the theme of the evening, rather than standing alone, marked out as different.

'Of course I will.'

'It's just that…' She made a glum little face. 'I got the feeling that you weren't very keen on the idea.'

The fact he'd almost hurt her feelings bothered him. She'd gone to so much trouble that he felt he owed her something. The sofa was only feet away, and he sat down on it, requesting she join him with merely a look. She frowned slightly, but sat down next to him, twisting a little to face him by tucking her right leg under herself.

'I can talk to you, Alice. You're so easy to be with.'

She didn't say anything to that—just gave him an odd look. He took a moment to look back at her and then let his gaze wander. He'd never be able to tell her this if he saw sympathy in her eyes. In fact her eyes in general seemed to be bothering him this evening. Over and over in the back of his mind he kept imagining her lids sliding closed, a small sigh escaping from her mouth. Although he'd asked her to sit next to him, he had the feeling now that it had been a bad idea. She was too close, too distracting.

His desk lamp was an obvious object to focus on—the sole source of light apart from the backdrop of the city—and he made himself focus on it as he prepared to talk.

For what seemed like hours he didn't say anything at all. Then, 'People think that going to a school like St Michael's is a blessing, a privilege. But that's only the case if you fit in.'

'And you didn't?' The soft concern in her voice almost made him falter.

He let out a little huff of a laugh. 'No. I didn't.'

He'd only just been tolerated in his first couple of terms. The fact that he was the class swot had earned him a few dirty looks. But he hadn't been about to dumb down for anyone— no matter what Daniel Fitzroy and his chums whispered about in their exclusive little huddle.

'Word that I was a charity case on a scholarship soon got around. There was a group of boys—a pack, really. You know how boys are.'

Out of the corner of his eye he saw her nod gently.

'Once they knew I had free school dinners too, they made my life a misery.'

▼ If offer card is missing write to: Harlequin Reader Service, P.O. Box 1867, Buffalo, NY 14240-1867 or visit: www.ReaderService.com ▼

NO POSTAGE
NECESSARY
IF MAILED
IN THE
UNITED STATES

BUSINESS REPLY MAIL
FIRST-CLASS MAIL   PERMIT NO. 717   BUFFALO, NY

POSTAGE WILL BE PAID BY ADDRESSEE

HARLEQUIN READER SERVICE
PO BOX 1867
BUFFALO NY 14240-9952

Send For
2 FREE BOOKS
Today!

I accept your offer!

Please send me two free *Harlequin® Romance* novels and two mystery gifts (gifts worth about $10). I understand that these books are completely free—even the shipping and handling will be paid—and I am under no obligation to purchase anything, ever, as explained on the back of this card.

❏ I prefer the regular-print edition
   316 HDL EYTQ 116 HDL EYNF

❏ I prefer the larger-print edition
   386 HDL EYT2 186 HDL EYNR

Please Print

FIRST NAME

LAST NAME

ADDRESS

APT.#   CITY

STATE/PROV.   ZIP/POSTAL CODE

Visit us online at
www.ReaderService.com

Offer limited to one per household and not valid to current subscribers of *Harlequin® Romance* books.

Your Privacy — Harlequin Books is committed to protecting your privacy. Our Privacy Policy is available online at www.eHarlequin.com or upon request from the Harlequin Reader Service. From time to time we make our list of customers available to reputable third parties who may have a product or service of interest to you. If you would prefer for us not to share your name and address, please check here ❏.

◄ Detach card and mail today. No stamp needed. ◄

H-R-09/09

He wasn't about to tell her how. But boys in smart public schools tended to go further than just words, and Fitzroy had been unusually creative in his approach.

'It all came to a head one day when one of the gang realised I was wearing one of his cast-off school blazers. My mum had been so chuffed to find it in a local charity shop because it was in such good condition.'

A wave of cold nausea swept over him and he clamped his mouth shut. He could still hear the taunts…

Charity case. Loser. Nobody.

So that time, instead of shrugging it off and ignoring their childish name-calling, instead of just picking himself up and refusing to lower himself to their level, he'd fought back.

It had been worth the weeks in detention and the lecture he'd endured from the headmaster—which, funnily enough, hadn't bothered him at all. Because the man had reminded him of his father. In a perverse kind of way he'd enjoyed it—as if it had been a rude gesture to dear old Dad by proxy.

Although Fitzroy and his buddies hadn't touched him again after that, the name-calling had continued. But after that day he hadn't cared. As for the blazer, he'd refused to put it on again—no matter how many further detentions he'd chalked up for not having the correct school uniform. He'd gone out and got himself a paper round, saved up and bought his own damn blazer. And he'd worn it with pride. Not that it had mattered to the bullies. They'd already labelled him. They'd already passed their verdict. He knew they would never change their minds about him, no matter what he did.

He didn't tell Alice any of this, but when he finally turned to look at her he knew that she knew. Not the details. But she knew about his sheer bloody humiliation. It made him unexpectedly angry to think the reason she understood was because she might have been through anything even vaguely similar herself. He just knew she understood it all—about not being able to live up to other people's expectations…everything.

When he spoke again, he aimed for levity. 'So—no—my memories of wearing other people's clothes are not good.'

She reached out and touched his hand. Such a simple gesture—nothing, really—but he felt his throat clog.

'Quality endures,' she said, looking deep into his eyes. 'It outlasts everything—fashion, prejudice, wrong opinions. In the end it proves itself, even if no one could see it for what it was at the time.'

He got the oddest feeling when she looked at him like that, her eyes all big and round, welling with moisture. He lifted a hand and wiped the underside of each eye with his thumb.

No, she mustn't cry for him.

Even though he was touched beyond belief by her honest reaction, he couldn't let her tears fall. He was scared of what he might do, what he might feel, if they did. So, instead of concentrating on her glittering eyes, he diverted his gaze to her mouth. The lips weren't overripe, but they were beautifully sculpted. Suddenly, he had the urge to *taste* again. And this time he didn't bother to ignore it.

CHAPTER SIX

ALICE felt a shiver run through her. Cameron was looking at her with his tiger's eyes and the warm glints seemed to glow brighter. Her heart began to pump faster than was strictly necessary.

Think oranges...

She started well. Aunty Barb was there in her mind, scrunching up her face and huffing with the effort of keeping the orange in place, but that image morphed into one of Cameron, his eyes dark and intense, concentrating on not dropping the darn fruit. And then he wasn't passing it to Aunty Barb any more, but passing it to her, coming towards her, his face getting close, lifting his jaw to meet hers so they could make the switch. And then the orange was gone, and it only took a minor adjustment in angles before lips were on lips and no one was trying to pass anything anywhere.

A tiny sigh escaped from her lips...

And then a jolt like a thousand volts shot through her.

It was real. Cameron's lips were on hers—kissing, teasing, coaxing. She was stunned at first, too overwhelmed to respond in any way, but then she couldn't help but kiss back, meet his lips and tongue with equal sweetness.

This was a kiss of fairy tales. Perfect in every way. It was warm and skilful and doing crazy, crazy things to her insides. Then suddenly it changed, deepened. Far off she heard something she could only think of as a growl, and a firm pair of hands closed around her torso and lifted her onto his lap.

And then—oh, wow—the hands didn't stop, but skimmed over the top of her cardigan, stroking, feeling. His lips moved away from her mouth, travelling along her jaw, down the side of her neck. She clung to him, ran her hands up his back and through his hair. What was he doing to her? What was *Cameron* doing to her?

Cameron.

The waves of tingles started to subside and cold reality crashed in, sweeping everything else away. This was Cameron Hunter. Software tycoon. The man who had to have not just everything but the *best* of everything. And while the kiss had been as near perfection as she could imagine it wasn't real— it was just a knee-jerk response at an emotional moment. She was Alice and he was Cameron. This was never going to be anything other than a moment of madness. A mistake.

Slowly she tried to extricate herself from his hold, but she was starting to discover he was pretty darn persistent himself. But it wasn't *her* he was kissing, not really. He'd just been feeling vulnerable…

'Cameron,' she managed to whisper between kisses, and pulled away enough to rest her forehead against his, her breath coming in short gasps.

She sensed rather than felt him smile, being too close to focus properly. 'Alice,' he breathed, and she just wanted to close her eyes and forget she had to stop this now—stop it before they did something monumentally stupid. He moved in to kiss her again but she managed to pull back enough to stop him reaching his target.

'Cameron... I have to...'

She didn't finish her sentence, too caught up in using his bewilderment to free herself and stand up. He looked totally dishevelled—and totally adorable, with a look of sheer confusion on his face. She'd bet not many people had seen *that* expression on Cameron Hunter.

She wobbled on her left foot, finding she'd put her weight on it awkwardly, but the momentum was enough to get her going—to get her backing away and heading for the door.

He jumped to his feet. 'Don't go.'

She bit her lip and shook her head, still backing towards the exit. 'I have to... You know that, don't you?'

And then she was running down the corridor to the lifts, leaving her handbag, her coat—everything—in her office. The lift door glided open and she bolted inside, pressed herself against the brushed steel interior. It seemed an age before the doors closed again, but no one came. No hand suddenly appeared on the edge to stop its progress.

Easy to be with? Easy to let go, more like.

He hadn't followed her.

He'd understood, damn him.

The opening ball for the new Orion Solutions headquarters was only hours away, and Cameron was in a foul mood. His PA had disappeared some time ago, squeaking something about an urgent errand, and hadn't returned yet.

Alice was also nowhere to be seen.

Why had he kissed her?

Alice had been nowhere to be seen since Thursday evening. And while his head told him she was probably at the new building—overseeing stage construction, briefing caterers—some other, more stubborn part of himself was taking it personally.

Even Jessica and Sierra had known the score. Nothing serious, no strings. When it was over, it was over. Women didn't just kiss him and then run. Basically women stayed, until he was ready to dismiss them.

Hah! That sounded so…so…pompous! He told himself he was being monumentally unbearable. So full of himself he'd really like to have given himself a slap. Had he really got that bad? Why had nobody told him?

Alice told you. When she looked at you with shock and horror and ran away. She knew what she'd done—what you'd become.

And, stupidly, all he could think about was that kiss. When he kissed other women it was all about playing a part, playing games—a subtle shifting of power back and forth, testing each other, seeing who had the most control.

He hadn't thought about any of that when he'd kissed Alice; he'd just *been*. Caught in the moment, thinking of nothing but how soft and right she felt pressed up against him, feeling nothing but a sense of completeness.

There was such an honesty about Alice. She didn't pretend to be something she wasn't. She wore what she wanted to wear, said what she wanted to say. She hadn't constructed some larger-than-life persona that she now had to live up to. So why had he?

It was as if he'd been forging ahead in one direction, never looking back, consuming everything in his wake, and Alice had made him stop and take a look over his shoulder at where he'd come from, who he'd once been. It had been a shock to see how much he'd changed. And now he couldn't switch off that knowledge. His other, truer self was like a ghost at his shoulder, whispering things in his ear, making him second-guess everything he now had and everything he'd attained.

Even this blasted ball tonight.

It now seemed like a three-ring circus rather than a stupendously elegant affair. The only reason he hadn't pulled the plug on the whole thing was that he knew he'd see Alice again there. Exactly why he wanted to and what he was going to say he wasn't sure; he just knew he had to see her.

Fighting a rather over-enthusiastic Coreen about hair and make-up was something Alice just wasn't up to at the moment. For the last forty-eight hours she'd been able to block out the memories of Cameron's lips on hers, of her flight headlong into the night, by working herself to a standstill.

But now everything was done, and the only remaining job was to get herself ready for the ball. Ready to be a knowledgeable, outgoing representative of Coreen's Closet. Meanwhile, her head felt like fudge.

It didn't help matters that she was standing in the middle of Cameron's office—his *new* office—now gloriously furnished. It was his personal space, and although he hadn't actually inhabited it yet, the rich intense colours—the midnight-blue carpet, the dark glossy wood of the desk and paneling, even a brass desk lamp identical to the one he had in his other office—made it impossible for her to ignore that the space belonged to him. She was in *his* territory.

Since Coreen and Alice would be on site all day, dealing with last-minute preparations, it had been agreed some weeks ago that they could get ready for the ball here. Because, tucked away behind a door in the panelling, there was a spacious bathroom and even a small dressing room.

Thankfully, even though she was on his territory, there was no sight of Cameron.

Thankfully?

What a lie! Every cell in her body was aching to see him again. Her brain was doing its best to argue back, but she thought it might be outnumbered.

So she let Coreen powder and brush and pluck and tease. That only made things worse. With nothing to keep her distracted, the rational side of her was overpowered by the side of her she'd tried to ignore. In her mind she started to regurgitate the events of that night in Cameron's *other* office.

Why had Cameron kissed her? Really?

She had theories, but no solid facts. Sympathy? Because they'd connected on some level? Had she finally got her wish and merely been the nearest available pair of lips?

She sighed, and Coreen, who was busy applying foundation, ticked her off for moving.

There was no future between a man like Cameron—he was probably a multimillionaire, for goodness' sake—and an ordinary girl like her. She was a second-hand girlfriend. And she knew for a fact that Cameron didn't do second-hand.

'Will you stop with the incessant sighing, please?' Coreen snapped. 'I almost took your eye out with the mascara brush.'

Alice blinked and came back to the real world. 'Sorry.'

Coreen was standing in front of her in a little black dress that was fifties restraint and pure sin all at the same time. It had a medium-length full skirt, a tiny, tiny waist, and a halter-necked bodice covered with sequin-studded chiffon. The four-inch red stilettos that finished off the look would make grown men weep.

She made a last little flourish of the mascara wand and stepped back to survey her handiwork.

'Fabulous. Even if I do say so myself.'

The only difference Alice could see was that her eyelids seemed to be weighed down with more gunk than usual.

'Next—the dress!'

Coreen was like a runaway train tonight. She suddenly dashed into the dressing room and Alice heard a rustling sound, then Coreen reappeared, looking smug.

'I've put my coat over the full-length mirror. No peeking until both the dress *and* shoes are on. You'll want to get the full effect.'

Alice just nodded, and trotted obediently into the little room. Her dress was hanging up in there, and she took it out of its protective cover and slid it on over the insanely expensive underwear Coreen had practically *made* her buy. Not that she'd actually needed to be forced that hard. Not when most of her bras were a little less than pristine white and held together with safety pins. She'd needed something to do this dress justice.

The dress went on easily, zipping up at her side, and then she reached for her shoes. Her Lucite-heeled shoes. The emerald of her dress reflected in the clear heels as she held them, making them seemed enchanted. It was the first time she'd felt worthy of wearing them—at least was wearing a *dress* that was worthy of them. She slipped them on and stood tall.

'You can come in now,' she said, staring at the fluffy collar of Coreen's coat draped over the full length mirror.

She turned slightly as Coreen entered, expecting to see a self-satisfied look on her friend's face—Coreen liked to think she was queen of the makeover—but found her looking slack-jawed.

'Wow. I mean…*wow*.'

Alice made a face. Coreen was such a drama queen. It was just the fact that for once she was wearing a dress and had a bit of…

Coreen whipped the coat off the mirror.

…make-up on.

Now it was Alice's turn to feel her jaw hit the floor.

'Told you!' Coreen had obviously got over her shock and was practically jigging from foot to foot. 'Told you it was *your* dress!'

The dress had *felt* exquisite as she'd put it on, but she'd been too busy stressing about the whole Cameron thing to think about how it would *look*. This was it. What Coreen had been talking about—the sum being greater than its parts. This *was* her dress.

The bias-cut satin floated over curves she hadn't even realised she had—maybe because she spent all her time hiding them rather than accentuating them with scary underwear. The colour was… It made her skin look like porcelain. And her hair… It was still as bright and fiery as ever, but it was parted on one side, falling in soft waves over her face, her long fringe almost covering one eye. Coreen had been mumbling about Rita Hayworth and Veronica Lake when she'd been doing it, but Alice hadn't really been paying attention. In this dress her hair…*worked*! She loved it. All of it. The hair, the dress, the shoes—especially the shoes.

'Thank you,' she whispered to Coreen's reflection in the mirror, suddenly finding herself all emotional,

Coreen came up behind her and gave her a quick squeeze. 'Don't you dare!' she warned. 'The ball starts in twenty minutes and I don't have time to do our eyes again. Come on—it's time to go downstairs and discover what last-minute snags have cropped up.'

They left the dressing room, and Alice went over to an abstract-looking chair to retrieve her handbag.

'Leave it,' Coreen said. 'We'll need both hands once we get downstairs.'

Good idea. She hadn't been quite sure how she was going to manage a clutch bag without looking as if she was clutching *onto* it. And, compared to the dress, it looked a little— well, downmarket.

'Showtime!' Coreen grinned at her, her bright red lips making her look like a Varga girl.

Showtime. Cameron's show. And, after all the work she'd done, hers too.

There was the last-minute snag—right there. It was her show, and it was time to step up and become the leading lady rather than just the understudy.

The exterior of the new Orion Solutions building was floodlit—the stark white lights throwing the carved stonework into relief, making it seem as if the columns rose into the sky and just kept going. Low box hedges framed the clipped squares of grass where only recently mere rubble had been, and as they arrived the guests marvelled at the transformation the indomitable Cameron Hunter had wrought. It was truly magical, they said. How amazing that this wonderful building had been under their noses all this time and nobody had ever paid it the slightest bit of attention.

They milled inside, continuing to exclaim at every little thing: the wonderful black and white marble floors, those darling Art Deco glass lights on the ceiling, and oh, *look* at that original dark wood!

Old Hollywood glamour.

The theme had been whole-heartedly embraced by those lucky enough to get an invite. Fabrics shimmered and swished, jewels sparkled, and everyone had an air of quiet self-importance. Some of the men had top hats and canes like Fred Astaire. One man had even gone to the trouble of putting on spats—although the general consensus was that they made him look more like a mobster than anything else.

The chatter increased as the guests wandered through the entrance hall into the atrium, and there everyone took a breath, a moment, and fell silent for a few seconds. Then they all started talking again, this time louder and more emphatically.

The lighting was deliberately low, and tiny white spotlights glinted in the glass roof like stars that had swooped down to see what all the excitement was about. Creamy white flowers were everywhere. At one end of the long rectangular courtyard was a wide stage, with chairs arranged in rows in front of it, and at the other end a large space for dancing and a forty-piece jazz band complete with a singer in a long white dress and an orchid tucked behind one ear.

But no one was dancing yet. That would come later—after the fashion show. For now an army of waiters offered trays full of colourful cocktails, and the topic of discussion became whether it really *was* better to have a martini 'shaken' and what exactly was *in* a Sidecar.

In the centre of the atrium was the fountain, flowing with water that fizzed and bubbled like champagne. It was surrounded by a thick black border in the marble tiles, marking out a square, and at each corner of the square stood a towering potted tree, leaves delicately draping themselves downwards as if reaching for the spray of the fountain. And there, standing under one of those trees, was Cameron Hunter, as calm and poised as everyone expected him to be. The perfect host. He greeted his guests warmly, remembering all their names, making them all feel welcome as he ushered them in to his little corner of the universe.

Cameron, however, was feeling far from calm or poised,

but he was—as always—doing an excessively good job of hiding the fact lest anyone suspect, lest anyone *judge*.

He turned, a smooth smile on his face, at the sound of his name. Only a microscopic twitch of an eyelid gave him away as he saw who had spoken.

'Daniel Fitzroy.' He omitted to say how pleased he was to see the man who'd made his schooldays a living nightmare, because it really wasn't true.

'Cameron.' The man grabbed his hand and shook it warmly. 'Thank you so much for inviting me—us.' He flicked a glance at the woman standing next to him, a small brunette with sharp eyes and an obvious bump under her stretchy black dress. 'We're really thrilled to be here.'

This was what he'd wanted—to see and hear Daniel Fitzroy bowing down before him, smiling like a weasel and pretending the past hadn't happened because he was so desperate to impress him. Cameron had always known that when this day finally came he'd have won. The memory of all those beatings would be erased and he'd be free.

And then, as if the universe had decided that granting his every desire tonight wasn't enough, and it was going to go ahead and grant his every thought as well, there she was.

Jessica.

Strolling towards him, resplendent in a long, deep pink dress with a bow that reminded him of a scene in a Marilyn Monroe movie—the one where she sang about diamonds. And Jessica hadn't scrimped on *those* either.

Why was she here? How had she got in? He definitely hadn't added her name to the guest list. But, then again, she was Jessica Fernly-Jones, and she never needed an invite to turn up to anything.

Despite the fact he hadn't seen her in weeks, and she'd not

been happy when he'd left her standing in her swish apartment with a scowl on her face and an 'ordinary' white diamond in her hand, she seemed perfectly at ease. She sauntered up to him and placed a soft kiss on his cheek before turning to smile at Fitzroy and his wife.

Cameron made the introductions. Everyone smiled at each other.

But, to his credit, Fitzroy's tongue stayed in his mouth, and he gave his little wife an affectionate squeeze. Bizarrely, that pleased Cameron. The small, serious woman at his side didn't deserve to be made to feel second-class, whatever he thought of her husband.

'Actually,' Fitzroy said in a low voice, pulling him to one side, 'could I have a word with you?' And he drew Cameron a few feet away, behind the potted tree and out of view of the guests spilling in through the doors.

The fashion show was due to start in fifteen minutes, and backstage was bedlam. Models were running around in their underwear, clothing rails filled every available space, and the clouds of hairspray necessary for some of the elaborate retro styles were starting to make Alice cough.

Even with all their friends from the market to help dress everyone and take care of the clothes it was madness. Alice took a moment to rest against a table and wonder why—for the thousandth time—she'd ever got suckered into doing all of this. She hadn't even managed to get out from backstage to see how the rest of the party was going. She was having to rely on reports from Stephanie, Cameron's PA, who actually seemed to be thriving in all the high-stress excitement.

Suddenly a hand clapped on her shoulder, and she jerked to a standing position.

'We've got an emergency,' Coreen said, a deathly serious look on her face.

It had to be at least the fifth time she'd made such an announcement this evening.

Coreen must have read her thoughts, because she added, 'No—this time it's a real emergency! One of the models, Amber—you know, the one with the hair?'

As far as Alice was aware none of their models was bald, but she let it slide.

'Well, she's throwing up in the toilets. Blaming it on a rice salad she ate at lunchtime. Boy, she does *not* look good! There's no way she can do the runway.'

Alice frowned. 'Can we give her dresses to some of the other models—share them out?'

Coreen shook her head. 'The changes are too quick. We'll have gaps in the show if we wait for them, and that will look unprofessional.'

Alice frowned even harder and put her thinking cap on. Everything was silent for a few seconds.

Hang on a minute. Coreen *lived* for drama. Why wasn't she relishing the moment, wringing her hands and gnashing her teeth? She turned to Coreen, who was still standing patiently next to her.

'You've got a plan, haven't you?'

A bright smile lit Coreen's face. 'I *have* got a plan!'

'And the plan is…?'

A manicured finger poked her in the chest. 'You. My plan is *you*.'

Cameron had followed Fitzroy behind the potted tree, too taken aback by the thought of Fitzroy wanting something from him to say anything. Now they were effectively in private Fitzroy shuffled a little, and couldn't meet Cameron's eyes.

'Actually, I wanted to apologise to you.' He glanced up, then returned to looking at the floor. 'I should have done it sooner, but…well, I just didn't. Perhaps I'm a coward.'

Yep. Pretty much what Cameron had always thought.

But Fitzroy suddenly squared his shoulders and looked Cameron in the eye—something Cameron didn't think he'd ever done before, not even when he'd been punching seven bells out of him.

'I want to apologise for the way I treated you at school. Back then…let's just say I had issues at home, and I dealt with it by taking it out on people like you—easy targets.' A genuine look of remorse clouded his features. 'Not that you were ever the soft touch I'd taken you for. You just refused to cower, no matter how hard I tried. In the end it just made me all the more determined to try. Not the right way to handle it, I know. But I'm afraid I just wasn't brought up to know any better. It was the only example I had.'

Cameron had come across Mr Fitzroy Senior over the last couple of years. He was a big cheese in banking, and Cameron wouldn't have liked even to work for the old goat, let alone be related to him. He bullied everyone he came into contact with. Being his son had to be a nightmare. From what he'd witnessed, nothing was ever good enough for that man.

He was suddenly reminded of his laser eye surgery—how everything had gradually come into focus, how he'd felt he was seeing everything in a new light afterwards. He looked at Daniel Fitzroy now and no longer saw an arrogant enemy too powerful to prevail against. Now he just saw the remnants of a boy who hadn't had the inner strength to cope with a vindictive father. How had he never seen how weak, how deserving of pity Daniel Fitzroy had always been?

And how had he never realised how similar he and the other man had been on the inside? How they'd both been damaged by their fathers' low opinions of them, even if they'd worn that pain very differently on the outside.

'I'm not that person any more, Cameron. I've changed.' He stole a look at his wife, who was deep in conversation with Jessica. 'And I want you to know that I am truly sorry.'

Cameron stood there, blinking at the man, the hot coals of the anger he'd been stoking for almost twenty years now smoking and hissing. He couldn't pretend he hadn't heard what the man had said, although part of him wished he could. Then he'd be able to go on hating, letting the furnace drive him forward. But Daniel Fitzroy had just made a genuine apology, and Cameron was not a man to ignore courage and integrity—even when it appeared in the most unlikely of places.

He reached out and shook Daniel's hand.

The other man breathed out a long sigh of relief and signalled with a quick glance at his wife that the deed was done. Silent communication. Unfortunately it gave Jessica an excuse to walk over with the woman, and she looped her arm in his and leaned into him, her large blue eyes wide and blinking—a little trick he knew she thought men found appealing, and once upon a time he had.

He honestly didn't object to talking to Daniel and his wife for the next ten minutes or so. The only drawback was that Jessica seemed to be attached to his arm as if she had octopus suckers, and he couldn't shake her loose without creating a scene.

Daniel's wife was obviously very much in love with him.

She looked adoringly at him as he spoke, her arm in his, her free hand rubbing the top of her bump almost constantly.

Cameron got the oddest feeling. He looked at the man Daniel had become and, while he wasn't sure they would ever be friends, he acknowledged how much he'd grown. He might not be the power-player his father was, but in Cameron's eyes it took guts to humble yourself before your greatest enemy.

In comparison, Cameron felt a little two-dimensional.

Where was his *own* adoring wife? His *own* promise of new life for the future? Nowhere. Because he'd dedicated his life to proving to the Daniel Fitzroys of this world that he was every bit their equal. And, for some totally unfathomable reason, he'd decided the best way to go about it was to amass as much money as he could and gallivant about town with useless creatures like the one currently affixed to his left arm.

Fitzroy hadn't let the past define him as Cameron had done. All these years he'd been fighting ghosts, fighting the shadows of bullies who had moved on with their lives, become men with lives and families. And now the anger was gone he realised there was a huge gaping hole in his life. The abscess had been drained, removing the fiery pain, and now there was nothing left but an ugly-looking hole. What was more, he had no idea how he was going to fill it.

Alice brushed Coreen's sharp little fingernail away. 'What do you mean *me*...? Oh, no! No way! Absolutely *no way*!'

Now the dramatics kicked in. Coreen threw her hands in the air and her voice boomed. 'Look around! Although we've booked models of different shapes and sizes, lots of these girls have exactly the same build as you. Poor old sick-as-a-dog Amber is virtually your body double.'

That might be true—sort of. But Alice knew for a fact that just because she'd been labelled a stick insect since her first day at school, just because she might *look* the part, it didn't mean she could actually model!

'Coreen, you must be out of your mind. You've obviously got me confused with someone who can walk more than five steps in heels without tripping over. And there are *stairs*…'

She ran to the back of the stage and peered through a gap in the scenery. The stage was flat enough—a wide rectangle, long side facing the audience, but they'd decided against the traditional T-shape of a catwalk, reasoning that if more space was needed for dancing later it would be better to have the models walk down a short flight of steps and parade along the marble floor before turning back and doing the process in reverse.

'Nonsense,' Coreen said, shoving her to the side to get a look herself. 'You'll be fine.'

Alice put her hands on her hips. Her future business was on the line here, and she wasn't going to muck it up with her clompy walk and complete lack of gracefulness. She couldn't go out there and have everyone looking at her—the whole room looking at her. Especially when *someone* would be looking at her, making her stomach flutter, her pulse race. There was a huge probability she would fall at his feet—literally.

She grabbed Coreen from where she was gawking at the other guests and made her look at her. 'This isn't a fairy story or a Broadway musical. The poor little insignificant nobody isn't going to step into the star's shoes and save the day! I can't do it.'

She waited for the fireworks, for Coreen to beg and plead and manipulate, but Coreen's eye was back at the crack in the scenery, and she was eyeing up the runway again. It didn't even look as if her fuse was lit.

'Hold that thought,' she said, and ran back to the dressing rooms.

The lights everywhere but on the stage dimmed, and a rustle of excitement went through the crowd. Gentle music—a little bit fifties, a little bit Italian—filtered through hidden speakers. The two banks of chairs with a central aisle weren't arranged to face the stage but each other, leaving a wide channel for the models to walk down, allowing the onlookers to get the best view of the outfits on display.

A lone figure stepped out onto the stage, and there was a collective gasp from the crowd. Cameron, seated in the front row, smiled. This wasn't usually his thing, but somehow this was different. He knew all the hard planning that had gone into it—every minute detail.

He knew, for example, that this wasn't really Audrey Hepburn, in a full skirt, flat shoes, prim white shirt and a scarf knotted round her slender neck, but a professional looka-like—one of a handful Alice had hired to make the fashion show a little more dramatic. By the looks of the people on either side of him, it had worked. 'Audrey' made her way down the short flight of four or five steps from the stage to the floor of the atrium and stayed in character as she walked, looking every inch the Hollywood star. A spontaneous round of applause rippled round the room. And then, as Audrey passed him, another model appeared—this one in a white dress with big red roses on it. A white scarf covered her hair and she was wearing sunglasses.

There was something familiar about that woman.

Coreen?

What was *she* doing modelling the clothes? That wasn't

supposed to be her job—although, by the reaction of a couple of men sitting opposite him, it really ought to be. It looked as if they were ready to leap off their seats and follow her wherever she went.

He was still puzzling as the *Roman Holiday* section ended and a small spotlight came up on a lectern at one side of the stage. A woman stepped into the pool of light and coughed slightly, before leaning a little too close to the microphone so it squealed back at her.

'Sorry,' a gentle voice said through the speakers, and every hair on every inch of Cameron's body stood on end.

He thought he was going to have a heart attack right then and there in the middle of his own party. It was Alice. And she was… Alice was… All he could think of. All he could look at. All he'd ever thought she could be and more.

The little vintage outfits she'd worn to the office had been cute, but this… Rich, dark green, swelling and curving and flowing around her. And her hair—her eyes! Dark, liquid, smoky make-up, and the deep crimson lips of a goddess. She turned round to ask someone behind the scenes something, and he really did think his heart had stopped for a second or so.

If the front of the dress had been spectacular, the back was…

He'd run out of words.

Two wide satin straps crossed over between her shoulder blades and travelled down, down, down until they reached the low back, just where the top of her bottom rounded away. Someone across the room wolf-whistled, and Cameron almost jumped out of his seat and started searching for him so he could knock his teeth out. But he managed to contain himself. Just.

She turned back again and tested the microphone, which was now behaving itself.

What was Alice doing there, staring at the audience, her eyes large and round?

CHAPTER SEVEN

OH, LORD, thought Alice. What I am I doing here?

Every eye in the room was on her. Every ear straining to hear what she was going to say. The only problem was she didn't *know* what she was going to say. They were expecting something witty and engaging. All she had in her head was garbled phrases.

Why, oh, why had she refused to model? What was so hard about strutting about a bit? At least that would only have involved being *looked at*. But with Coreen stepping in for Amber she'd been forced into the role of auctioneer. Now she had be looked at *and* say stuff.

The plan was to auction off the pieces straight after their section of the show, so they were fresh in people's minds. The first model—Annie, the Audrey lookalike—stepped out onto the stage and struck a relaxed pose, her hands clasped behind her back in a girlish manner, and it instantly reminded Alice of stills she'd seen from *Roman Holiday*. She could almost hear the music—almost see St. Peter's Square and the Colosseum, feel her own heart beating with the first love of a shy girl escaping from her life of duty for a few precious days.

And then the words were there, inside her head. She took a deep breath and leaned into the microphone.

'Ladies and gentlemen, imagine yourselves in Rome at the height of summer, zipping through the crowded streets on a Vespa, the wind in your hair, the swell of freedom in your heart…'

If anyone had asked Cameron what each piece of clothing had sold for, he wouldn't have been able to tell them. He hadn't been paying attention to the numbers, only to the soft clarity of Alice's words, the way she moved her hands when she described a piece, the smile she bestowed on the winning bidders. Cameron wasn't a man who took his time deciding what he wanted, and he knew what he wanted right now— one of those smiles.

The final section of the auction was progressing—the one with the Marilyn lookalike. Evening dresses in all colours of the rainbow, made out of all kinds of fabrics: lace, satin, taffeta, organza…

Not that Cameron knew anything about fabrics, but he retained the information because it had been delivered in Alice's voice.

She was amazing. The whole audience was eating out of her hand, leaning forward to catch every syllable she uttered. Coreen would have been a great auctioneer, parting the punters from their money with her outrageous curves and cheeky banter, but Alice… Alice was something else. Totally different.

A unique way of looking at things, he'd said. And now she was putting that gift to work with marvellous effect.

She didn't sell the clothes, she sold the *dream*—the very essence of all those classic movies. She didn't just describe each item of the sale, but she put it in context, creating a little story about each blouse, each handbag, each dress, until the guests were desperate to outbid each other for just a little bit of that fantasy. He wasn't sure, but he thought some of the pieces had gone for ridiculously high sums.

He'd been so busy caught up in her spell he realised that he'd forgotten to bid for anything—had forgotten to earn one of her smiles. Not that he'd have known what to bid for. Whatever would he do with a stole or a pill-box hat? It wasn't as if he had a woman in his life to shop for any more. And now the last bid had been made, for a metallic embroidered sheer dress similar to the one Marilyn had worn in *Some Like It Hot*. That dress he remembered all on his own. What red-blooded male wouldn't?

But it wouldn't have done. He wouldn't have bought it anyway, because it would have looked so wrong on her...

Oh.

Mentally he'd been looking for something for Alice, and he hadn't even known it.

He frowned and berated himself. He should have known, should have made more of an effort, because now everything had been sold and his chance to surprise her with a gift, to say thank you for the wonderful job she had done, was gone. A little voice in his ear urged him to stand up, *make* one of the happy bidders give something up for him. He could do it. It was his ball, his building, his night, and he knew he could make any outrageous demand he wanted and people would scurry round to make it a reality.

But he didn't.

In his imagination he could see the look of disapproval on Alice's face. She wouldn't accept anything he obtained for her by those means anyway. So, although it was almost painful, he kept his mouth shut and his bottom in his seat.

Silence fell, and Alice removed the microphone from its stand and walked to the centre of the stage.

'We have one last piece of vintage clothing to auction off this evening…' She did a little twirl and Cameron felt his stomach clench, the blood pound in his ears. 'This Elsa Schiaparelli dress.'

A murmur of excitement rumbled around the room.

'It's a deep emerald satin evening gown, designed in 1938 for…'

The details blurred in Cameron's ears. He didn't need to know them. This was Alice's dress. No one else should ever be allowed to wear it—and he was going to make sure they wouldn't.

He was going to buy it for her.

And, in the process, he was going to earn himself one of those smiles.

It had been a spur-of-the-moment decision. Coreen had said she could auction this dress if she wanted to, and while it was the most beautiful thing she had ever worn and was ever likely to wear, when would she *really* ever have the chance to wear it again? After tonight she'd be back to blue jeans and T-shirts, bashed-up old trainers and her brother's fleeces.

The amount the auction had managed to raise for the local charity so far this evening was truly amazing, much more than she'd ever imagined possible, and she'd rather that this exquisite dress put an extra couple of hundred pounds in the kitty rather than sit in the darkness at the back of her wardrobe doing nobody any good.

'I'm going to start the bidding at one hundred pounds.' The reserve was five hundred. Surely it would go for much more than that. 'Do I have one hundred pounds?'

Instantly a hand shot up, the woman half rising out of her seat.

'One hundred pounds to the lady over there. Do I hear—?'

'Two hundred.'

Alice stopped mid-flow and turned in the direction of the voice. Not just *a* voice, but *the* voice. Her eyes met Cameron's. He was looking straight at her, his expression completely open. What on earth would Cameron want with a dress like this?

She couldn't look away as she said, 'Do I hear—?'

'Three hundred.'

This was a new bidder. She acknowledged a woman in a mink stole with a nod, but before she could open her mouth that deep, sexy log fire kind of voice said, 'Five hundred.'

And that was how it carried on. Every time someone else bid, Cameron topped it. She stopped looking at the other bidders and felt a gentle heat rise to her cheeks as she kept her focus on him. Only on him. He was smiling too. A secret smile. A shared smile. One that connected them in such a way that the rest of the room melted away, became like background music.

She really must remember to breathe. It was interfering with the whole auctioneer thing. But the way that Cameron was looking at her—as if she was the only thing in his field of vision—seemed to be having an effect on her ribcage, making it squeeze tight around her lungs.

He's bidding for your dress. For you.

Don't be so stupid, she told herself. That would mean... Well, it would mean all sorts of things it was impossible for it to mean.

But that warmth in his eyes, his smile...

She knew it was true even as she accepted a bid of a thousand pounds from the original bidder and the whole room gasped. Cameron just smiled, and Alice knew his lips would open again, that he would add another hundred.

And he kept ~~doing it. But~~ Cameron ~~was~~ not a patient man, even though his nonchalant expression all through the auction almost fooled her. Hard lines of irritation at being constantly trumped started to show around his jaw. When the bid reached one thousand eight hundred, he snapped and stood up.

'Ten thousand,' he said, in his low, controlled voice, daring anyone to go higher.

Nobody did. They were all too shocked, busy whispering about his outburst, and before anyone with enough capital behind them had enough thought to bid against him it had gone. It belonged to him.

She belonged to him.

And, while the crowd dispersed in a collective hunt for another champagne cocktail before the ball proper began, she stayed centre stage and he stayed in his seat. They were grinning at each other.

She would wear this dress again. One day soon. She didn't know when or where, but she knew one thing for sure: Cameron would be at her side.

Cameron found himself in the midst of a group of businessmen, all congratulating themselves on their foresight in investing in his company and haw-hawing over each other's off-colour jokes. He listened with only half an ear while he scanned the vast atrium for any hint of a green dress.

He hadn't seen her since right after the fashion show, when he'd been but a few steps away from her and then Coreen had bustled her off backstage to do something urgent. She'd smiled at him, raised her eyebrows in apology, and since then he hadn't even had a glimpse of her.

When he was able, he excused himself from the group of men and went in search of her. That was the problem with being the man of the moment. Everybody wanted to shake his hand, or have a word, or slap him on the back and remark on his ten-thousand-pound bid.

He started at the edge of the dance floor, which was packed, all the time looking, his eyes searching out a particular shade of emerald. And then he saw her, talking to some of the guests who'd been unlucky in the auction. He recognized the woman in the fur who'd bid for Alice's dress. She wasn't looking very pleased, and she was trying to press something into Alice's hand.

Cameron tried to get to her, but he kept having to dodge people as they circled the fringes of the dance floor. It seemed whichever way he decided to go people deliberately stepped in his path, causing him to zig-zag. Once he'd cleared a particularly obstinate clump of left-footed dancers he looked to the space where Alice had been standing—but she was gone.

Damn.

The fashion show had finished almost an hour ago and it was nearing eleven o'clock. He needed to find her before the party ended.

Something rather round and rather solid barrelled into him, almost sending him flying—and that was no mean feat. He twisted round to find a portly man in a white dinner jacket mouthing apologies at him.

He'd just planted his feet solidly on the ground again when he became aware of someone standing behind him, waiting for him. Some unknown instinct told him it was a woman. Slowly, very slowly, he turned to face her.

Alice stopped dead, and her skirt swirled round her ankles then fell into perfectly spaced folds.

There he was, maybe only twenty feet away, and she

watched as he turned without seeing her and faced the most stunning woman she'd ever seen outside the pages of the fashion magazines. If she'd needed a definition of glamour, this woman was it. Blonde. Tall. An eye-popping figure. In other words she was everything Alice was not. And she couldn't even fault her for her carriage or her dress sense. She held herself as if she was entitled to get everything her heart desired, especially the man she had set her sights on, and there was nothing cheap or nasty about her recreation of Marilyn's pink dress from *How To Marry a Millionaire*. Even from this distance Alice could tell it was beautifully made.

The blonde snaked her hand around Cameron's arm and reached down to twine her fingers with his, then leaned in close to whisper something in his ear. His back was to Alice, so she couldn't see his expression, but he leaned forward and whispered something back. Just the thought of his lips being that close to another woman, so she'd feel his breath tickle her ear, made Alice's stomach instantly freeze with jealousy.

The way was open now. A clear path between her and Cameron. She could just walk up to him, tap him on the shoulder, smile and cut in…

But she didn't

She watched her moment slide away, watched the crush of the crowd push Cameron and the blonde further away from her until they had disappeared. Stupid, she knew. But she didn't want to have to stand next to the vision in pink. She didn't want Cameron to make comparisons. Alice never did well in that kind of situation. She had never been anyone's first choice.

Later. When he was alone. When he wouldn't be distracted, dazzled… Maybe then she'd have the chance to see if that warm smile was still in his eyes for her. She turned and walked in the other direction, her sense of euphoria deflating as quickly as an old wrinkled party balloon.

Later seemed as if it would never happen. Alice found herself at the beck and call of all sorts of people for the next half an hour. The bar was running out of ice, someone had twisted their ankle trying to foxtrot and needed the first-aid kit, the clothes sold at the auction needed to be hung properly and labeled, so they could be claimed by the right owner. As organiser of the evening Alice had to deal with all of these things, and although she managed to delegate, something else often popped up to suck away her time.

The large, square white-faced clock above the main entrance to the atrium showed that it was twenty to twelve, and she hadn't been able to find Cameron anywhere since she'd dealt with her latest emergency. Alice had the horrible feeling that if she didn't find him tonight that warm smile for her would disappear from his eyes and never come again.

All around her people were dancing. Some twirled expertly, like Fred and Ginger, some merely held onto each other and attempted to match the beat of the music. Alice's brisk walk slowed as she took in the sights and sounds around her.

She watched as a couple near her swayed. They were so taken up with each other that they weren't even really dancing any more. They weren't moving in time with the music, just moving in time with one another. His hand held her firmly round her waist; one of her hands was cupped at the back of his neck, claiming him. Their free hands were knotted together and laid against his chest, and they were just staring into each other's eyes. After a few moments, he kissed her nose. She sighed and rested her forehead against his and they shuffled away.

One dance, thought Alice. That's all I want. Once dance.

Surely that can't be too much to ask for—not after all the hard work I've put in?

As if on cue, she saw him. The undulating sea of dancing couples parted long enough for her to catch a glimpse of Cameron. He was dancing with someone. Slowly. Gently.

Her heart stopped.

But then he turned his partner and her pulse kicked into life again. It was an older lady he was with, her silver hair festooned with a long black feather tucked into a twenties headband, and Cameron was smiling indulgently at her.

Once again Alice made her way towards him, picking up speed now, but just before she was close enough for him to hear her call his name the blonde materialised, cutting in and leaving the older woman to smile politely and then look daggers at her back as she steered Cameron away.

But Cameron looked up over the blonde's shoulder and his eyes locked onto Alice's. He gave her the barest of smiles—one that said *Sorry. I'll be with you soon…*

Alice exhaled as he disappeared out of sight again. The warmth had been there—the smile—and she knew without a doubt that when the song ended he would make his excuses and come and find her.

Suddenly, for the first time in her life, Alice had the burning urge to go and check her lipstick.

Being quite familiar with the ground floor layout by now, she knew that a ladies' room was just outside the side door nearby—one that other people might not know about. It would be cool and quiet, and she could check her make-up and gather herself together before Cameron found her. She slipped out through the door and hurried down a short corridor.

When she actually got in front of a mirror, she realised that she couldn't have done anything about a lipstick disaster anyway. The little tube of deep berry-red Coreen had lent her was in her bag. And her bag was in Cameron's office. But it turned out she needn't have worried. The lipstick had lived up to the advertising campaign and was still virtually tattooed on. By the looks of it she'd still be trying to scrub it off next Tues—

The door creaked and Alice instinctively straightened. It seemed a bit vain to be caught nose to mirror, examining her reflection. She ran her fingers through the long wave of bright hair that half covered her face before glancing in the direction of the person—the woman—now hovering just beyond her field of peripheral vision.

Oh. It was *her*.

She turned to leave, not really wanting to share a confined space with the blonde—Cameron's blonde—but found her blocking the exit, one hand on a curvaceous hip. The other woman looked her up and down, the tiniest of sneers twitching her lips into an ugly shape.

'Excuse me,' Alice said, and moved to pass her.

But Blondie didn't budge. She licked her glossy lips and gave Alice a slow, predatory smile. 'I think we need to have a chat, darling.'

Dah-ling. On her lips, the word sounded positively vicious, despite the fact that her voice matched her appearance—cool, cultured. Expensive. Alice felt her hackles rise, but she wasn't about to give this woman the advantage by letting her irritation show.

'A chat about…? And who are you, anyway?'

She laughed—a soft, husky sound. 'Oh, I think you know the subject we both have in common. And I'm *Jessica*.' She raised her eyebrows, clearly waiting for a response.

Alice didn't have one to give her. She had no idea who *Jessica* was—other than that she'd been wrapped around—

'Jessica Fernly-Jones,' she added, as if it should mean something.

Alice just stared back at her, and waited for her to get whatever it was she wanted to say off her ample chest.

'Cameron and I...we've been seeing each other for months. We're very...*close*, if you know what I mean?'

Alice's stomach began to churn, but she pulled her abdominal muscles in tight. 'And what has this got to do with me?'

That laugh again. It probably drove men wild, but it was as soothing to Alice as nails down a blackboard.

'Now, now. Don't be coy with me, darling. We're both women...' Her gaze fluttered down to Alice's chest and back up again. 'We can be frank with one another.'

Jessica Fernly-Jones could be as frank as she liked. It didn't mean Alice would return the favour.

'He's a very attractive man, as I'm sure you've noticed...'

Alice flushed, then a rush of anger at her own involuntary response compounded the problem. Jessica gave her a long, knowing look.

'He uses it to his advantage, you know—to get what he wants. Whether that be sealing a deal, crushing his competitors...' a split-second glance in the direction of the atrium was all it took to add a little venom to her next words '...to see a project finished to his high standards. But he never gets involved. He always moves on, looking for that elusive perfect woman. You *do* know that, don't you?'

Alice forced her lungs to expand, even though her rib cage felt horribly tight. The action helped her keep a lid on her anger.

Jessica gave her a look of mock-sympathy. 'Oh, poor girl...'

Girl? From the looks of it Miss Fernly-Jones was only a year or so older than she was. That was it. She wasn't listening to any more of this.

She could hardly believe that Cameron could get involved with someone like this. But she knew just from the body language she'd witnessed on the dance floor that Jessica was telling the truth—she had a history with Cameron. Whether it was anything more than ancient history remained to be seen.

Once Dawn from the market had learned who Coreen's Closet was working with, she'd tried to inveigle her way into the project by being useful. She'd sent Alice e-mail after e-mail with information about Cameron she'd found on the internet. There'd been articles from the business pages, but also snippets from the gossip columns—and in every entry he was pictured with a different woman, each one more stunning than the last. That was obviously what appealed to him, and even in her current state of fancy dress Alice knew she just didn't qualify. Cameron liked eye-candy.

She didn't want to believe he was that shallow, but she couldn't ignore it. He was driven, but damaged. After his revelations the other night, she knew that he was capable of all the things Jessica had just accused him of—but she understood why. How pathetic was it that the knowledge just made her ache for him more, made her want to soothe his pain? Why couldn't she just harden herself and walk away?

Jessica had been watching her face, and now a look of self-satisfaction spread a smile across her lips.

Alice pulled herself tall. 'Well, thanks for the tip, Jessica. Now, if you don't mind, I'll be on my way…'

This time Jessica shifted position to let her pass, and Alice celebrated a very minor victory in these horrible few moments of her life. She hadn't let Jessica win. The woman had thrown all her ammunition at her and she hadn't let Jessica Fernly-Jones see her crumble. Alice felt Jessica's eyes drilling holes into her back as she headed for the door. Her fingers had just closed round the handle when Jessica released her parting shot.

'It's a beautiful dress.'

Alice just pulled the door open. This conversation was over.

'I'm looking forward to wearing it.'

Just go. Don't react. Walk away.

The tug of curiosity was too strong—like the morbid fascination that caused drivers to slow down and rubberneck on a motorway when there'd been a pile-up, even though they knew what they saw might disturb them. She looked over her shoulder. Jessica was walking towards her, her mask of civility discarded, half hanging off.

'That's right, darling. He bought it for *me*. Didn't you see me sitting next to him, egging him on?'

Alice gasped. At the time she'd been too busy looking at Cameron and running the auction to process the other details her eyes had been sending to her brain, but now the information arrived, breathless and apologising for its lateness.

Jessica with her hand on Cameron's forearm. Jessica whispering into Cameron's ear...

Jessica ran a hand carelessly through her platinum waves. 'Cam's always said he likes me in green.' Her eyes narrowed as she came to stand virtually nose to nose with Alice. 'Or should I say he likes it so much he prefers to see me *out* of it?'

Alice felt sick. She didn't know what kind of game this woman was playing, but even the thought of her naked with Cameron turned her stomach to ice. And she couldn't even dismiss the images rushing through her brain as nonsense, because at some point recently they probably had been reality. She yanked the door open and left Jessica standing alone in the ladies'.

There was only one way she could respond to all of this information. Alice did what she did best.

Alice ran.

CHAPTER EIGHT

THE cold air hit her hard. The heavy glazed door swung closed behind her and she dragged in a breath and folded her arms around herself, trying to rub flat the goosebumps that appeared instantly on her upper arms. The imposing building towered above her, the lines of the giant sunburst above the door harsh and foreboding in the floodlights.

Blast. Her coat. It was upstairs in Cameron's office.

Even though it was bitterly cold she wouldn't have thought twice about leaving it there, but it wasn't just her coat she needed. Her bag was up there too, and without it she had no phone to call a cab, let alone the means to pay for it.

She sighed and headed back indoors. At least she wouldn't have to pass through the atrium to get her things. She could just nip up the winding stairs and be out again before anyone saw her. Not that anybody was likely to be looking for her but Coreen, and the last Alice had seen of her she'd been chatting up one of the saxophone players on his break.

It seemed to take for ever to clomp up the three flights of stairs in her shoes, her Lucite heels announcing her presence to anyone who cared to listen. So much for 'nipping' anywhere. But there was no other noise in the echoing stair-well. She was pretty sure she was alone.

Finally her telltale shoes were silenced by the thick dark carpet of Cameron's office. Alice realised from the soft glow coming from the open doorway that, although she'd turned the office lights off when they'd left earlier, she'd forgotten the one in the dressing room. Not wanting to announce her presence in the office to all the partygoers in the atrium, who would be able to see the light in the windows if they looked up, she decided not to hit the main switch. She only needed to find her bag, and her eyes were becoming accustomed to the dark already. The light from the dressing room would be enough.

Now, where had she left it?

Oh, yes…by that funny-looking chair with the chrome frame and wide leather straps. It looked very stylish, but it had to be the most uncomfortable thing she'd ever sat on. Obviously Cameron didn't want any of his visitors getting too relaxed.

Cameron.

Just the thought of him made her sigh.

She shook her head and went in search of her bag. But it wasn't on the chair. Where had it gone? Alice squinted in the dark and thought she made out a shape on the floor. It must have dropped through the leather straps. She crouched down and reached for the dark lump. Her fingers met velvet, and she picked up the slightly tired clutch bag. She was just straightening her legs when she heard a door graze the carpet.

Someone was coming. Please let it be Coreen. Please don't let it be…

The world started to spin faster and faster. He was silhouetted in the doorway by the bright lights of the hallway, and then he stepped into the shadows and the door swung closed behind him.

Even though purple blobs were filling her vision, multiple

imprints of Cameron's outline in negative, she knew he was looking at her.

'You can't leave yet, Alice.'

What was it Jessica had said? Oh, she couldn't remember the exact words, but the truth had hit home, and the squeeze of her heart at the thought brought the stinging sentiment behind them rushing back. Something about Cameron being very charming when he needed to be—when he wanted something from you.

The ball was almost over. What on earth did he need from her now? Couldn't he just let her go before she made a fool of herself? She hugged her bag to her midriff. Her heart and her head were telling her completely different stories, and she needed time to work out which one was fibbing.

'I—I have to.'

I must.

She had to leave now, before he guessed. Before he took pity on her.

Cameron stepped forward. 'No.'

Such a firm word, in such a firm voice, but with such an undercurrent of gentleness. His voice had always affected her, and now it called tears forth from her eyes. Let him be gruff, let him be impatient and bossy. Please, please, don't let him be kind.

He started to walk towards her, and Alice wanted to scurry away and grab her coat, but she stayed rooted to the spot. It was as if he was holding her there just by the sheer weight of his stare.

She broke eye contact.

That was better. Shakily, she started in the direction of the dressing room, where her coat was hanging. She'd be fine as long as she focussed on the little diamanté buckles on her shoes, if she didn't look him in the eye.

'Alice.'

A soft command.

He reached for her. His fingers brushed the bare skin of her arm, and it was as effective at stopping her in her tracks as a rugby tackle. Her chest rose and fell as she concentrated on each little rhinestone on her buckles in turn. But it couldn't shut out the awareness of him, of how he was circling her, how he'd come to stand in front of her.

'Don't leave. Not yet.'

She made her first fatal error. But with fatal errors one was all that was needed. She looked up at him. His eyes were dark, holding a riddle.

He took the bag from her hands and dropped it on the desk.

'Come.'

Cameron's voice was low and soft. When he got assertive it reminded her of the big crackling flames of a log fire, but right now it was more like the little tiny flickering ones. They were the dangerous flames. Their little licks fairly *seduced* the logs into ash.

He didn't take hold of her hand, but she followed him as if he had, tugged along by him as he led her to the balcony. They ended up at the railing, staring down at the party still in progress below them.

'Look,' he said.

And she did look. From up here, suspended above the dance floor, the view was magical. The lights… The colours… Gold and silver, red and purple, turquoise…jade. All those beautiful ballgowns set against the stark black of hundreds of dinner jackets, all spinning and turning. It almost seemed as if it wasn't just individual couples moving, but that every person, every pair, moved in harmony, creating shifting kaleidoscopic patterns on the wonderful mosaic marble floor.

She'd been so frantically busy tonight, so caught up with a thousand little details that she'd forgotten to step back and look at what she'd managed to achieve. The atrium looked amazing—everything she'd pictured when she'd scribbled all those notes and made all those phone calls had come to life. It was real—happening. As if she'd conjured it up by dreaming it.

She'd done it.

The evening was a success.

The soft sounds of the big band—saxophones, lazy trombones and the husky voice of the singer—floated up above the heads of the guests and drifted into the great glass roof, from where they echoed back again, just enough to make the sound seem distant, other-worldly.

'I asked you for "distinctive". You gave me more than that. *Much* more than that.'

Ah, that was what this was. A thank-you speech. Well done, little Alice. Big pat on the back. You finally did something that made people sit up and take notice. Good luck for the future. See you again some time…

But if that was all this was, why was his mere presence having such an intoxicating effect on her? Why was her heart pounding, her breath coming in shallow gasps? And why had his hand covered hers, his thumb now circling the back of her hand?

'I haven't seen you dance once this evening. Will you dance with *me*, Alice?'

This couldn't be real. It had to be something to do with this evening, this strange sense of…*fairy tale*…that just refused to leave her alone. But she let him pull her to him, too weak-willed to walk away. Too weak-willed to run this time.

Didn't he know why she hadn't danced all evening?

It had to be him. No one else. And all evening he'd been so distant, always just beyond her fingertips and out of reach.

He's still out of reach, she told herself. *Don't kid yourself that just because his arm is around your waist, pulling you close, because his chin is only inches from your forehead, because you can smell the fresh cotton of his shirt mixed with aftershave, that he will ever be truly yours. This is just now. This is just for tonight.*

I won't be a fool, she told herself back. I won't forget. But I'm not stupid enough to rob myself of this memory either.

He'd been wrong when he'd listed all the things she'd given him. She'd given him *everything*. More than just a great party, a good idea, value for money. He had her heart, her soul, her very last breath.

The band started to play 'The Very Thought of You', and gently, almost so she didn't notice, he began to lead her, dance with her, moving with his signature efficient grace. Her heart was reaching out for him with a persistence that became a bittersweet ache. It was too late now. She might have been able to walk away with her pride intact if he hadn't come up here, if he hadn't offered her a taste of what life might be like if fairy tales happened every day.

She'd fallen in love with him. Just like that. Even though her brain told her it was all a spell woven by the magic of the night—magic she'd manufactured herself.

Thank goodness he wasn't ostentatious with his dance moves—dipping her, twirling her out and in again. Thank goodness he kept her pressed close against him, where she could feel his breath in the roots of her hair, where she could stare at his lapel and avoid his gaze.

Maybe it hadn't been *just like that*. Maybe, like Lewis Carroll's Alice, she'd been falling for such a long time she could hardly remember when the downward journey had begun. All that had happened now was that she'd finally had the shock of hitting the bottom.

She loved Cameron.

She loved his quiet integrity, his single-minded focus. She loved the way he surprised himself sometimes by laughing out loud.

The song changed to something even mellower, and Cameron's circling movements became smaller and smaller— until they were no longer dancing, just holding each other.

It was almost too beautiful to be true up here amid the echoes of love songs, her face now against his shoulder, just the remnant of a sway keeping them from stillness. But it had to end soon. The knowledge settled in her like a stone sinking to the bottom of a pool. He'd pull away, look into her eyes and say goodnight. Goodbye. She was easy to say goodbye to.

But he was kind. He spun the moment out for her, and instead of releasing her his arms came around her completely, and she felt the soft pressure of his lips against her forehead.

She'd wanted a magical memory, but this was almost too intense. It wouldn't warm her in the future when she thought back to it; it wouldn't comfort her. It would burn, leaving her raw for ever, leaving her wanting relief, with none to be had.

'Alice? Look at me.'

She tasted salt on her lips. Quite how the tears had fallen there she wasn't sure.

'I…' She didn't get any further, but gulped the words away.

This time he didn't say *no*. His gravity didn't pull her. She knew she could keep her eyes on her feet and run out of there if she wanted to and he wouldn't stop her. After a few moments she tilted her chin up, but kept her gaze fixed on his chest, then slowly she raised her eyes to meet his.

He didn't look hard tonight, all angles and planes. He looked torn, almost sad. There was a softness in his eyes she'd never seen before. That feeling of *connection* hummed between them. It grew and grew until it pounded in her ears— until the only way to drown it out was to lean closer and closer and closer…

The first kiss was nothing more than the merest touching of lips, a promise. There was such purity in it, such sweetness, that Alice forgot all her stern words to herself about holding back. She ran her hands up his arms, around his neck, and dragged Cameron closer. She kissed him as if her life depended on it.

Maybe it did.

She'd never felt this overwhelming need to touch and taste a man before. She couldn't have stopped herself even if she'd tried. And Cameron…

His lips wandered down her neck, across her collarbone. His hands settled around her waist, his fingers brushing against the smooth fabric of her dress, creating a slow, sliding friction that drove her even crazier than she already was.

It had never been like this with anyone else. With Cameron she forgot to plan each move of her hands, her lips. She forgot to think about what she could be doing better, or to worry about not being sexy or experienced enough. With Cameron she just dissolved into the moment, losing her sense of self completely and then finding it again, reflected back to her in each brush of his lips, each caress of his hands.

This man in her arms was always so sure of himself, so sure his every move, every decision was the right one, and to feel him pull her tighter against him, murmur her name, to sense that he was just as lost in this as she was made her soar. Cameron desired her. He wanted her. With an intensity that was so strong it almost scared her.

And she loved this man. This was everything she'd ever dreamed of. Except...

Except in the dream he didn't just desire her, he hadn't just got caught up in the heat of the moment. In the dream he loved her back.

One miracle in an evening was enough to expect. She'd never realised Cameron *really* shared the intense attraction she felt for him until tonight. That should be enough. Asking him to love her too... Well, that was just being silly.

She put her hands on his upper arms, bracing herself slightly, and pulled away. Not enough to look into his eyes, but enough to be able to talk without just giving in to his magnetic pull and kissing him again.

'Cameron, what is this? What are we doing?'

Cameron, as always, was more comfortable with actions than words, and he ran both hands down her back. The feel of them through the satin of her dress was even more delicious. He let them come to rest on the curve of her hips. Alice was very tempted to just shut up, close her eyes and stop asking difficult questions. Questions she wasn't even sure she wanted the answers to—because that would only break the spell once and for all.

Oh, she knew he wasn't about to go back to Jessica Fernly-Whatsit. Cameron might be fickle with his women, but there was no way he would be up here with her on the balcony, kissing her the way he'd kissed her, if he still had anything going with Jessica. He just wasn't that kind of man.

But she wasn't sure he was the kind of man who could give her all she wanted either. He kept himself locked up so tight, used his anger to power him forward. She didn't even know if he'd be brave enough to let that shield down and give all of himself to someone. And, even though this was Cameron she was thinking about, Cameron who could so easily be the one she trotted around after for ever, she wasn't prepared to accept anything less than the full package from him.

It was high time she was somebody's first choice rather than just being second best.

Something was bothering Alice. He could tell. If only he had some of that intuition women were famous for, then he'd be able to work out *what* was making her brows pinch and her mouth set itself in a firm little line. He didn't like it when her mouth did that. It made her look very determined. And he'd much rather she was using her lips to kiss him again rather than produce an expression that put a niggle in his gut. He didn't know why, but he had the oddest feeling he wasn't going to like what she had to say next.

Maybe he could convince her to soften that line, to put the curves and arches of her lips to a much more pleasurable use. Maybe, just maybe, he could wangle it so they didn't need to talk at all. He was pretty sure he could convince her to sink against him again, to run her small fingers over his skin, to breathe tiny sighs of desire into his ears. And he didn't think he'd have to say a word to do it.

He moved his hands upwards from where they were still resting on the swell of her hips and circled her waist. She was so slender his large hands almost met in the middle, and somehow that made him feel even bigger and stronger. She seemed such a tiny, delicate thing in his hands, yet he knew that her response to him had been anything but delicate. In fact, it had completely blown him away.

Other women *tried* to be sexy when they were with him. They tried to live up to the idea of going out with an eligible millionaire bachelor as if they had to impress him to keep him interested. And, to be honest, he required that of them. Wanted them to be the fantasy women they both pretended they were. Even women like Jessica.

He hadn't wanted to know and be known. He hadn't wanted to get close enough to anyone to let them see who he really was, to expose himself and make himself vulnerable. The temporary nature of his relationships had been the perfect solution. Move on to the next one, promising himself he was looking for the pot of gold at the end of the rainbow, when really he was just running, running…

But with Alice it was different. She didn't do any of that with him. And that was what made her so wonderful and so confusing at the same time. She was sensuous and sexy because he knew every touch and every kiss was real, true, honest—as if she was undressing her soul for him.

Being a red-blooded man, the twin thoughts of 'undressing' and 'Alice' in close proximity made his core temperature rise. And thoughts of undressing led to thoughts of that dress, of sliding the wide straps off her shoulders and watching the heavy fabric sink to the floor.

She was looking at him, and underneath the film of caution in her eyes he saw matching heat, matching need. It was all the encouragement he needed to bend his head and deliver a kiss that was hot and sweet and hungry. Alice was still for a split second, and then she joined him, as if she'd been resisting but just couldn't hold back any longer. The knowledge just drove him even further overboard, made him want her even more.

What is this? What are we doing?

He knew exactly what they were doing. He knew exactly what he wanted and how he pictured this ending. And in his head the scenario involved that long leather sofa, him and Alice stretched along the length of it, and the sexiest dress he'd ever seen—his dress now, as he hadn't officially given it to her yet—in an emerald heap on the floor.

He continued to kiss her, continued to blot out that concerned look in her eyes, and his hands skimmed her torso until they found their way under those silky straps. And then he was gently walking her backwards off the balcony and into the office.

After the third step Alice froze.

He wasn't a man to push in situations like this. In reality he'd never needed to. But that *something* that was bothering her, that he'd tried to wish away—it had just stamped its foot down hard, and it wasn't going anywhere until it had been dealt with.

Slowly he eased his hands from under the straps, careful to leave them in place, and dragged his lips from Alice's. But he was unable to resist returning for one last brush, one last taste, before he pulled away fully.

Just to keep his itchy fingers out of temptation's way, he ran his hands up her neck until he was cradling her head and just waited. This had to be about what Alice wanted.

This had to be about what Alice wanted.

The phrase repeated in his head.

How shallow, how *horribly* shallow, had he been up until now? All his relationships with women up until this moment in time had been about what *he'd* wanted. Not in the sense that he'd bullied or domineered—far from it. He'd always treated the women in his life well. But only because it had suited him to do so. Because he'd gone out with those women to boost his status, to prove to the rest of the male population that he could have what they could only dream about. This evening had turned all of that on its head.

First Fitzroy, showing that Cameron didn't have the best

relationship by far, that he only had a poor imitation of the real bond Daniel had with his wife. And now Alice—sweet, lovely Alice—turning him inside out with her honesty, with her fragile power.

So, instead of persuading her any further, he stepped back, gave her space.

'Alice? Tell me.'

He knew he had to be the one to speak first, because he had been the one who had cut off the talking earlier. How he knew this he wasn't quite sure. This being real, being open, was all a bit new to him. He was just going to have to feel his way.

The pain he saw in her eyes made him wince.

The fear must have shown on his face, because her expression hardened.

'I can't have a fling with you, Cameron. You know you can make me stay if you want to, but I'm begging you—let me go. Let me walk away. I'm not one of your perfect women.' She gave a dry little laugh and shook her head. 'I wouldn't even know where to start!'

Then she surprised him by walking towards him and running her slim fingers down the length of his tie. When she reached the point at the bottom she flipped it over and parted the seam a little, revealing a brightly coloured lining.

'Here she is,' Alice said quietly. 'The other night I forgot...'

The blobs of colour all at once started to make sense. It wasn't just a swirling abstract pattern but a picture in the lining of his tie—a pin-up, to be exact. Betty Grable-style, with rolled hair, bright red lips and a skimpy white halter top. She was winking at him.

'This is the kind of woman you need. Always ready, always glamorous, never having an off day. Who cares if she isn't real? She'll never ask anything of you, never ask you for a piece of your soul. In short, she'll always be your perfect woman.'

She let the tie go and patted it back into place.

'They're very collectible, you know. Ties like these. If you ever decide you don't want it you should be able to get a nice price for it.' She smiled brightly at him even as her eyes brimmed over. 'Coreen's Closet would give you a really good deal.'

Despite his promise to himself to give her the space she wanted, he found himself reaching for one of her hands. 'I don't want you to be like—'

She pulled her hand away. '*Please*, Cameron!' Tears shimmered on her lashes, ran down her cheeks.

He hated himself for being responsible for them, for not being enough of a man for her to stay for.

'I need to go home,' she said in a flat voice.

'You can have my car. It's—'

She shook her head. 'All I need is my bag and my coat.'

He fetched her coat for her while she got her bag, and then she walked out through the door. But before she left she turned slightly and whispered one last thing. 'Thank you…for not making me stay.'

For the longest time Cameron just stared at the back of the door. He wanted to go and drag her back, explain. But that would be the worst thing he could do. Instead he flipped his tie over and took a look at the hidden woman inside. That wasn't what he wanted at all!

He was through with fake two-dimensional women. He wanted someone who made him feel alive—someone who made him *feel*, full-stop. Someone like Alice. Someone exactly like Alice.

But he couldn't blame her for not realising he'd changed—

not when he'd only just cottoned onto the fact himself. But he had to try and make her see…

He thought of Alice making her way home alone, tears in her eyes. He thought about the limo parked outside, ready to whisk him anywhere he wanted to go, anywhere he commanded. She'd asked him not to stop her leaving, but he hadn't said he couldn't follow her, had she? He had to give this one last chance.

He had a lot to offer a woman. And he was going to offer it all to Alice.

By the time Alice emerged from Cameron's office she discovered the ball was drifting to a close. Music still played, but it came from speakers. The band had been booked to play until midnight and they were now packing up. Only a few dozen people were left in the atrium. Some were still dancing, most were chatting, and every few seconds another small group peeled off and headed for the exit.

She deliberately didn't look up as she scurried across the vast space, past the stage and beyond, into the mayhem of the backstage area. It was all quiet now. Clothing racks stood empty, everything having been packed away by an army of helpers, and the only noise was a scuffling coming from one of the corners.

It was Coreen, sitting on one of the vintage suitcases—battered sky-blue leather with a chrome trim—that she'd brought some of their stock in. She was trying to persuade it to close, with the help of her curves and a little gravity. She looked up and saw Alice.

'Give us a hand, will you? I can't get the blasted thing shut.'

Alice dropped onto the suitcase next to her, too soul-weary to do it gracefully. It did the job, though, because Coreen leaned forward and clicked the fasteners into place. She grinned at Alice.

'Now, as long as it doesn't decide to spring open before I get in the cab, I'm all set.'

Alice sighed. 'Is that offer of sharing a cab still open?'

One of Coreen's eyebrows twitched upwards. 'Course it is.'

An even bigger sigh escaped from her lips and Coreen slung an arm round her and squeezed.

'Hey, come on. We did great! You're just having the slump after the adrenaline high. Get home, have a hot chocolate to pump up your blood sugar, and you'll be fine.'

Post-adrenaline slump. That was what this was, was it? Nothing to do with having just walked away from the man she was in love with? Good. She'd be fine by morning, then.

Only she wouldn't.

Love wasn't the comfortable armchair she'd always imagined it to be. It wasn't safe and warm and fluffy. It was scary and painful and heart-stoppingly exciting. Nothing like the sanitised version she'd inflicted on the men in her life.

Was this what Paul felt when he looked at Felicity? This heart-thumping, brain-frying, all-body tremor-inducing thing? She understood it now. Why he'd left. Why he'd had to follow it wherever it took him if he had a chance of finding someone who could make him feel like this, who felt the same way about him. Good luck to him. And she really meant that.

Coreen stood up, grabbed her hand and tugged her upright. 'Cab's due in five. We'd better get outside.'

Alice just nodded. Then she looked at the suitcase. 'Shouldn't that have gone in the back of Dodgy Dave's van with everything else?'

'Are you nuts? I've got all the costume jewellery in here,

padded out with a few scarves and a mink cape. I'm not letting dear old Dave get his mitts on this!'

It made sense.

She let Coreen yabber away as they walked to the front of the building and climbed into the waiting cab. Alice sat numbly in the back as they nipped through the quiet back-streets to her house.

She'd done the right thing. She'd had to run when she had.

If she'd been weaker, had given in to Cameron's pull, then she'd have ended up in a terrible mess—her heart squished beyond recognition and no good to anyone, not even second-hand. That didn't mean that it didn't hurt like hell, but it did mean that one day, when she found someone who thought she was everything a woman should be, she'd have something to love him back with. She just hoped her poor heart had recovered by then—because it seemed to have a terminal case of something at the moment, despite all the sensible things she'd done to protect it.

At least she'd have her new business to concentrate on. From what Coreen had said they had been inundated with requests for more of the same kind of merchandise from some very wealthy potential clients. She was even talking about finding a shop to lease in a better neighbourhood than they'd looked at before—something a little more upmarket.

Coreen lived closer, so it made sense for the taxi to drop her off first. And, horrible as it might sound, Alice was quite relieved when she and her blue suitcase were gone. She was able to drop the fake smile, stop all the nodding, and just slump in the back seat of the cab.

Back to real life now, Alice. Pull yourself together. The ball was a success. Coreen's Closet is going to take off. You've got the whole world at your feet.

Thinking of feet, she looked down at her Lucite shoes. They were still as fabulous as ever, but they were both still accounted for. Cinderella she was not—even if she'd seemed to track of that for a while back there. No, it had all been smoke and mirrors, spotlights and glitter balls. Now it was time to get back to the real world. Time to turn back into a pumpkin.

CHAPTER NINE

THE limo didn't have any problem trailing Alice's taxi. Cameron drummed his fingers on the arm rest as he watched the cab stop and let her out. He paid careful attention to which path she went up in the narrow car-lined street filled with redbrick terraced houses. As soon as he'd pinpointed the right front door he was out of the car and knocking on it.

But it wasn't Alice who answered, but a short guy in a curry-dribbled T-shirt. He didn't even bat an eyelid when Cameron asked for Alice, even though it was half past one in the morning.

'You'd better come in,' he said, opening the door wide. 'We're not quite sure what to do with her.'

We? And what was the matter with Alice?

Cameron followed the man into a living room dominated by a large flat-screen TV and enough high-spec audio visual equipment to make any geek's heart soar. A battle game of some description was paused on the TV—a large, sharp-toothed monster frozen in mid-air, about to land on a blood-smeared dragon. The remains of a takeaway were littered across the carpet, along with a couple of empty cans of cheap beer. And in the middle of all this clutter and stale-smelling furniture was Alice, in her dark green ballgown, looking as beautiful as ever and sobbing her heart out.

He walked over to her, crouched down and took her hands. She didn't even flinch, too miserable even to be surprised to see him. She held up a shoe and gulped.

'I broke my shoe,' she said and just started crying all the harder. 'My beautiful shoe…'

Cameron was a bit wrong-footed by that. Maybe his male ego was bigger than it should have been, because he'd thought—had maybe even hoped in a warped kind of way—that she'd been crying about *him*.

He took the shoe from her. The clear glass-like heel was hanging off.

Puzzled, he looked at Alice again. He knew girls liked shoes, but *this* much…? And he hadn't ever suspected *Alice* was one of those girls. But until a couple of weeks ago there had been a lot of things he hadn't suspected about Alice. How funny and strong-willed she could be. How resourceful and determined.

'They're just shoes,' he said, sitting down next to her. 'You can get another pair.'

Alice looked at him as if he'd just insulted her mother. 'I don't *want* another pair! I want this pair. But it's broken and I don't know how to fix it and I'll probably never be able to wear them again.' She paused to take a deep gurgling sniff. 'And I'll never find another pair like them. I might never find another pair *at all*! And then I'll be *shoeless* for the rest of my life. Old and lonely and…and…shoeless!'

Cameron looked at Alice. He hated seeing her like this. If he could, he would hunt down her heart's desire and give it to her on a silver platter. Gently he prised the other shoe from her grip and put the pair down on the floor beside him, avoiding a foil curry container with an oily slick in the bottom.

If Alice wanted these shoes, and these shoes only, then he would have them repaired—whatever the cost. And if they couldn't be repaired he'd scour the globe for replacements.

He took a deep breath and hoped the universe was still in the mood for granting wishes tonight. Because he really wanted to convince Alice to give him a chance, to let them explore whatever this thing between them was.

'Alice, I'll take care of the shoes. Whatever you want, I'll get it for you.'

She looked up at him, her gaze flicking between his eyes, searching for the truth of his statement.

'What I want is to know what *you* want, Cameron. Why are you here?'

Such a simple question. So hard to answer. Partly because he wasn't sure how to put it all into words, and partly because he didn't know if he was brave enough to do it if he could. He settled on asking for something concrete.

'I would like to spend more time with you. I don't want…*this*…to be over.'

He'd had it with *temporary*.

A strange combination of suspicion and surprise clouded her eyes.

'Why? Why me?'

Because I can't stop thinking about you. Because I love being with you. Because I have a feeling that if I don't see you again something inside me will shrivel up and dry out.

Those words sounded so lame inside his head—like bad dialogue from a cheesy chick-flick. He couldn't say them, even if it was true. He reached out and took one of her hands in his.

'Because you deserve to be treated like a princess.'

There—that was much better. Women always liked to hear things like that.

So why did Alice swiftly pull her hand out of his? Why did her chin jut forward just a little?

'I'm not a princess and I never will be. Don't kid yourself.'

Frustration started to form a cloud in Cameron's head. Why was she being so stubborn? She was being ridiculous. Didn't she know how sweet and funny and clever she was? Who had been telling her otherwise? He'd like to find that person and make them eat their words—swiftly followed by their teeth.

She got up and walked away from him, and when she could go no further, when she had reached the corner of the room, she turned and faced him, one hand on her hip.

'Did you love Jessica?'

Cameron stiffened. Where the heck had *that* come from? And what did Jessica have to do with him and Alice? Had she been whispering in Alice's ear? Knowing *dah-ling* Jessica, she'd have had her claws out if she'd had the opportunity. He needed to put this right—make Alice see sense.

'No, I didn't love her.' Sometimes, towards the end, he hadn't even liked her—despite the fact she could be very charming company when she wanted to be. It struck him that even after four months of on-and-off dating he hadn't really known Jessica at all. She too put up a front—a bulletproof sensuality that deflected everything. And it had never bothered him. Maybe she was as much a coward as he was. He wondered what she was really like behind her fun-loving party-girl persona. Not because he was interested in her in a romantic sense any more, but because he was suddenly certain there was more under the surface than he had ever seen, had ever bothered to look for. 'I'm not sure I even knew her very well.'

He'd hoped it would put Alice's mind at rest, but somehow his response had just made her frown all the harder.

'Then what was it that made you want to go out with her in the first place? If that isn't a really obvious question...'

He tore his eyes from hers and looked across the room to the TV screen. The monster was still frozen; the dragon was still blood-smeared. He didn't want to open up and tell her this. Now he looked at his behaviour it all seemed so pathetic. Alice would think badly of him if he told her the truth—that he'd been afraid, that underneath all the hype he was still a quivering coward. He almost laughed out loud. Oh, God, the bullies had been right after all.

But she'd send him away if he didn't say *something*, so he'd just have to try and make it sound not too awful. He couldn't bear it if she looked at him in disgust, if he saw her opinion of him change.

'It's hard to explain...' He tried to tell her that it hadn't been as heartless and cynical as it sounded. Even though he hadn't been in love, he'd honestly been *infatuated* with the string of women he'd dated. It was just that the shimmer of perfection that had attracted him to them in the beginning hadn't seem to last. And just as he was starting to lose interest he'd spot someone else and he'd be off again, the whole cycle repeating itself.

As the words poured forth he felt himself hollow out. It was a horrible feeling because the space wasn't left empty. A cold wind of fear rushed in to fill the void.

'It wasn't a calculated thing. It's just...'

'It's just that you were living up to your name.'

He turned to look at her. 'What?'

'Hunter. You obviously love the thrill of the chase.' She looked at the floor. 'Not so keen on the *keeping* of what you've won, though. Always on to the next thing—bigger and better...'

Up until now that part of his character had always seemed a positive thing—it was how he'd achieved so much success so quickly—but the way Alice said it... She sounded so blank, so hopeless.

He got up and walked over to where she was standing.

'None of that matters now.' Inside, his stomach began to pitch. 'I don't want Jessica. I don't even want someone else like her. I want you.'

'This isn't real,' she said. 'It's the evening, an adrenaline rush, a *moment*...'

Wasn't real? How could she say that? The very air around them was pulsing with authenticity. Couldn't she feel it? For the first time in his life he was seeing things clearly.

'And I can't do this if all it is going to be is a moment.' She fixed him with a serious look—one that made his pulse stutter. 'You know what I'm talking about, don't you?'

He nodded.

He didn't want just a *moment* either. But the implications of that were making his head spin, filling his stomach with a fear he just didn't want to name. The opposite of *temporary* was *permanent,* and he'd never really planned on 'for ever' with anyone. He didn't know if he could do it even if he wanted to.

'I think...I think there's something there between us, Cameron. But I'm not sure there's any mileage in it.' She nodded, more to herself than to him. 'And I'm ready for mileage—for long distance.'

He wanted to say he was too, but after what he'd said about his previous relationships the words sounded a bit empty as they echoed round his head. Now he was getting desperate. And when Cameron got stuck in difficult situations he fell back on tried and tested methods.

He wanted to tell her about the life they could have

together, the life she deserved. All the best restaurants. And she wouldn't have to wear anything second-hand ever again. He'd buy her *haute couture*—the sort of thing other people would be bidding for at auctions in fifty years time. She would be the first person to wear the clothes that would be *tomorrow's* vintage. But he didn't say any of this, knowing he would be digging his own grave.

She looked very glum, resigned.

'One evening—that's all I'm asking for.' For starters. Once he'd dazzled her, in true Cameron Hunter style, she would change her mind. She *had* to.

'I don't want just one evening, Cameron.'

Her chest rose and fell, and she stayed silent for the longest time—as if she was inwardly struggling with herself. In the end she walked over and opened the living room door.

Once again he found himself in the position of wanting to argue back but not really having a leg to stand on. He didn't know if he was ready either, but he *wanted* to be ready. Surely that had to count for something?

'Wait there,' she said, and disappeared upstairs. She returned a few moments later. But now she was in stripy flannel pyjamas and she was holding the green dress in her arms. She held it out to him. The tears were gone—along with most of her make-up—and she looked pink, puffy, and slightly soggy. Cameron wanted to kiss her.

'Before you go,' she said, 'I thought I ought to give you this. It's *your* dress really.'

'But I bought it for you.'

She took a moment to think. He could tell she was doing that, because her forehead did a very characteristic crinkle and she looked at the floor. After a few moments she raised her head and looked at him, seemingly having reached some kind of decision.

'I know you did.' She held it out to him. 'But this isn't me. Not really. The woman who wore this dress tonight isn't the real Alice. This—' she indicated the flannel pyjamas '—is the real Alice. And she doesn't fit into your world. You'll see that in the morning,' she added. 'You'll be thinking more clearly then.'

He knew that anything he said would just make her resist him even harder. He'd definitely underestimated this quiet determination of hers. It was as hard as diamonds. He took the dress from her, and she gathered up the shoes and placed them on top of it in his arms.

'Please go, Cameron.' Her voice was barely a whisper as she stood there, not looking at him, holding the door wide. 'I'm begging you. Just go.'

He couldn't bear the fact he was doing this to her, so he just had to do as she asked. But he felt as if he'd left a piece of himself behind when he walked out through the door. He was halfway down the street before he remembered his limo, parked across from Alice's house. His driver was fast asleep and he decided not to wake him. He'd give him an extra bonus to compensate for the ridiculous hours tonight. So, while Henderson snored softly, Cameron sat in the back of the car and watched as the lights went out one by one in Alice's house. He wondered which was hers.

She'd said he'd see sense in the morning, and maybe he would. Until then there was nowhere else he wanted to go. Not even with the whole city at his feet.

Alice had had a thoroughly disgusting night's sleep. When she'd finally been able to drop off she'd spent the whole night terrorised by images of random things waltzing through her subconscious—jewel-coloured dresses, doner kebabs, and shoes. Lots and lots of shoes.

Cameron had pushed her too much last night. Too much too soon. And the only thing she'd been able to do to give herself some time and space to sort all this out was to push back. She knew he thought he meant what he was saying, and she so wanted to believe him, but…

The street lamp across the road flickered off now dawn was breaking. The orange strip of light she'd been staring at on her wall disappeared.

Cameron was not a good bet. He was a relationship magpie, and she wanted a future—with a man who wasn't always going to be scanning the horizon for something better. She didn't need a high-flying playboy who got bored easily. No.

She was being unfair to Cameron, thinking about him like that. He wasn't heartless. But she didn't think he was ready for love and commitment. When she'd said she didn't want just 'a moment', she'd seen the doubt written all over his face. Not that he'd ever say so; he'd rather die than admit he was deficient in any way. His pride wouldn't let him. And while he kept feeding that pride, while he *needed* to be Cameron Hunter, software developer and millionaire bachelor, while he needed to keep proving himself, he'd never be ready. She'd never be enough for him.

She breathed out and stared at the ceiling. No woman could *ever* be the perfect being he was hunting for. The knowledge gave her an odd sense of relief, and she rolled over and hugged her pillow, wondering if she'd be able to doze off now she seemed to have settled a few things in her own mind.

Her room was directly over the front door, and slowly she became aware of a gentle but very persistent knocking.

There was no hope Matthew or Roy would answer it. They never emerged from their rat holes until well after midday on a Sunday. But Alice was fed up with being the only one who did anything in this house, and she decided she wasn't going to haul herself downstairs to answer the door, but would open her window and just yell down at whoever it was to clear the hell off. It was eight o'clock on a Sunday morning, for goodness' sake. All civilised people were asleep or at the very least indoors at this time of day.

She lifted the catch on the window and shoved the sash upwards, ignoring the drips of condensation landing on her head.

'Why don't you just—?'

Another drop of water hit her just behind her left ear as she stared into Cameron's upturned face. He didn't smile at her, just indicated the large paper bag he was holding with a nod of his head.

'It's morning. I'm seeing things more clearly. Can I come in, please?'

Alice just continued to gawp at him. Had he really taken what she'd said so literally? She was too surprised to argue with him, and discovered, despite her earlier rebelliousness, that she wasn't about to have a shouted conversation with him from her window so all the neighbours could hear. She'd seen a few curtains twitch already.

She shut the window, tiptoed downstairs and opened the front door. Cameron pushed the package in her direction.

'I brought you breakfast,' he said.

It smelled heavenly. Without looking inside she knew it was warm buttery croissants and strong coffee. Just what she'd have fetched for herself if she'd thought about it. She didn't say anything—just led the way to the kitchen.

He was still wearing the same clothes as last night. That dark suit... But the tie with the hidden pin-up was missing, and the top button of his shirt was open, making him look even more devastatingly sexy because now he had a slightly dishevelled un-Cameron-like appearance.

But he smelled the same. Of aftershave and fresh cotton. Possibly the most intoxicating scent ever.

All the memories of being pressed up against him on the balcony came flooding back, and when Cameron placed the package on the counter and pulled her close for a kiss she didn't have it in her to push him away.

It was even better than she remembered. Better because now it didn't just feel as if it was something she'd dreamed. He was here, in her kitchen, and he still wanted to kiss her. She wanted to hope, she really did, but the thought of him looking at her as Paul had done the night he'd dumped her squashed any lingering optimism flat.

She ended the kiss and stepped away from him, clasping her hands behind her back lest they get any funny ideas.

'I don't see how anything's changed since last night,' she said. 'It was only a few hours ago.'

He set about unpacking the croissants and coffee, getting plates and knives. He'd even brought butter—real, unsalted French butter.

'I've been thinking,' he said. 'About what you said. But you can't just push me away without giving me a chance. I won't let you.'

He stopped what he was doing and looked at her, *really* looked at her. All of a sudden it wasn't Cameron the big-shot businessman looking at her, but an unsure boy, full of fire and doubt and insecurity.

Not fair.

She could resist the armour-plated persona, but not this…

The backs of her eyes stung. He had her heart already.

What more did he want from her? To play with it for a while? To try it on for size to see if it fitted? No way.

The 'old' Alice, the Alice who had let Paul use her as his personal doormat, would have gone along with whatever the man in her life said in an effort to please him. And there was no doubt that pleasing Cameron at this present moment would reap some very rich rewards for herself too. It would be so tempting to just fall into step with him, to live a charmed life for a while, but 'new and improved' Alice—the Alice who had appeared in the last couple of weeks since she'd started working with him—who liked to push back against him, just wasn't ready to lie down and surrender.

Maybe because more was riding on this. She'd never felt this way about anyone else before, not even when she'd been running around after the men in her life, doing everything in her power to convince them she was worth staying around for.

Why had she never thought to ask herself if *they* had been worth the effort? She'd foolishly just pursued her dream of finding someone to love her without asking if they were capable of it.

This time she needed to know.

Because if she was just going to be Cameron's 'stopgap', until somebody better came along, she couldn't bear it. If she watched his interest fade while she ran herself into the ground trying to convince him otherwise, if he appeared one day with a sheepish expression and told her there was *someone else*, she would never recover. She couldn't stand thinking about him with someone else after he'd been with her. For the rest of her life she'd torture herself with images, thoughts of Cameron looking deep into some other woman's eyes as he had hers last night, of Cameron's hands on the curves of someone else's body. She had to protect herself.

She drew in a breath to steady herself, and was surprised at the way her body shuddered as she did so.

'Cameron...we just can't be together. We're from different worlds.'

He had it in him to dig his heels in hard, and she prepared herself. He was going to fling objections at her, and she was going to have to bounce them right back.

'Don't be daft. Your brother almost married Jennie. We were almost related once. Your parents are still on my mum's Christmas card list, for goodness' sake.'

Alice's shoulders sagged. She was just going to have to try another tack. But he just mowed down every roadblock she erected against him until she felt desperate, trapped. After half an hour of fending him off, both of them still firmly entrenched in their positions, Alice was exhausted and Cameron was rapidly losing his cool. Just as she thought she only had enough energy left to flop onto a stool and cry into the kitchen counter, an adrenaline surge hit her and she came out fighting.

Cameron watched her march to the back door and then march straight back again. Her breathing was fast and shallow, and he suddenly realised she was right on the edge of coping with this whole situation. To be honest, he wasn't far behind her. They were getting nowhere.

He'd never really seen Alice angry before—worked up, exasperated, but never shimmering with rage as she was now as she paced around her poky little kitchen. This wasn't going to plan at all. He'd been hoping to placate her, to make her see sense, but with every word that came out of his mouth she'd just hardened herself further and further.

'Give it to me straight,' he said, running his hand through his hair. He could take it—he hoped. 'Tell me why you won't agree to even one date. I just don't understand.'

She gave a dry laugh. 'I bet you don't. But I've got news for you, Cameron Hunter. There are some things you can't buy, and I'm one of them.'

'I don't want to—'

She flung her hand wide, sweeping past the bag full of breakfast things that neither of them had touched. 'What's all this, then? And how about the dress? You think that you can click your fingers and everything will fall into your lap. But I'm not going to be yours just because you've made some spur-of-the-moment decision that I should be.'

Where was she getting all this stuff? Was that really how she saw him? Or was this just desperation talking?

Alice's pacing had brought her close to him, and he reached out and gently pulled her into his arms. For the longest time he just held her there, feeling her warm breath against his shoulder. And then, when he felt some of the tension released from her shoulders, he pulled back to look at her.

'I thought you knew me, Alice,' he said softly.

The stillness that followed, the sadness, was worse than her pacing and heated words had been. She reached up and touched his face, her eyes wet.

'I *do* know you.'

The last of Cameron's defences slowly slid into a jellified heap. Standing before her now, looking into her eyes, he felt as raw and unprotected as he had the first day the bullies had jumped on him.

His voice was patchy and low when he finally managed to speak. 'This is all new to me. I don't *do* this. I don't do begging. Why do you think I'm here on your doorstep on a November morning? I'm begging you to give me a chance.'

She looked so horribly torn he wanted to pull her back into his arms and pretend he'd never let the words out of his mouth.

Her eyelashes swept downwards and back up again, and one slow tear rolled down her cheek.

'You don't know how hard it is for me to say this…' She bit her lip and took a moment to regain her composure, pressing her mouth into a crinkly line and crumpling her chin. 'I'm an ordinary girl and I belong with an ordinary guy. You…you always need the best—of everything. And I'm really not sure I can ever be that for you. Oh, maybe you'd think that for a couple of months, but…'

He opened his mouth to deny it, but she pressed a finger to his lips.

'Even if by some miracle I could be that for you, I've come to the conclusion that maybe—' Her voice cracked and she went very still. 'Maybe you're not the best thing for me. I don't think you're ready, Cameron. I don't think you've got it in you to give me what I need.'

The tears were slipping down her face now.

'I so want to be wrong, but I don't think I am.'

He started to speak, but she silenced him again.

'I know you're growing, learning, but I've been hurt too. I can't take the risk. It's all or nothing with me, and I'm sticking to my guns this time. I won't settle for anything less. I won't settle for second best.'

He felt his jaw clench under her touch.

'You're calling me second best?'

He'd thought he had a lot to offer a woman, and he'd offered Alice even more than he'd realised he had, and she was still telling him it wasn't enough—*he* wasn't enough.

She hung her head. 'I'm calling it how I see it, Cameron. I'm just telling you the truth.'

He felt his anger like a physical heat. Even Alice must feel it radiating towards her. And then he turned and left. It was the only thing he could do to stop himself losing it completely. The front door banged so hard behind him it bounced open again.

He was livid. Maybe because it was easier to be rip-roaring angry than feel the rawness her words had caused.

Alice didn't think he was good enough.

She'd declared herself judge and jury and sentenced him. Completely unfair. He hated this feeling—had *always* hated this feeling—the sense that he'd been held up to some invisible measuring stick that he could never quite catch a glimpse of and been found wanting.

For years he'd managed to evade this sensation. He'd made sure everything he did and everything he built was designed to eradicate it. And now Alice was telling him he was *wrong* for having done that.

Even though it was Sunday he went to the new offices and stomped around a bit, made some phone calls and barked at people. Not that there were many people around to bark at. He had to go hunting, and then he found only cleaners and people from the staging company removing the last of the evidence of last night's festivities. It was all very unsatisfying. But slowly his anger cooled, leaving him with only a dragging feeling that made him think unaccountably of the tree at the edge of the cricket pitch at his old school—the one he'd climbed up to hide in when Fitzroy and his gang had been on the prowl.

Alice had delivered her verdict. He had to deal with that.

That afternoon and most of that evening he pondered what she'd said. And in the end, no matter how painful the admission, he'd had to admit she'd been right—partially.

He'd been so busy creating a perfect front to present to the world he'd forgotten it was just that—a front. And in his stupidity he hadn't paid nearly as much attention to the man inside the iron shell. Nobody else questioned it. Everyone else saw the hype he'd created about himself and was deluded by it. But not Alice.

The man she'd met again a few weeks ago hadn't been ready for a real relationship. He'd been proud, arrogant, completely up his own backside. But she'd changed all that. He wasn't that same man any more. Why was that? What had she done to him?

The answer popped into his consciousness like a random fact suddenly remembered—like when you racked your brains for an answer to a general knowledge question that you knew you knew but just couldn't recall. Then, days later, it would come out of the blue, while you were doing something mundane and totally unrelated, and you'd wonder how you could have forgotten it when the answer had been obvious all along.

He loved her.

He loved Alice. Every molecule of his being vibrated with it and he knew it was true—just the way he knew the earth was round, the battle of Hastings had taken place in 1066, and the tallest mountain in the United Kingdom was Ben Nevis.

And now he *knew* that he knew he loved Alice, he also knew that he was ready to stand by her side for the rest of his life. This was gut knowledge, not a flimsy scientific theory that would be disproved by the next bit of research. The certainty of it was like a rock inside him.

Ironically, he wasn't sure Alice was ready to hear it.

He wasn't the only one who was battling with a pursuing fear. *I've been hurt too…*

Her words came back to him. Who had hurt Alice? Who could possibly hurt her?

Alice was sure what he felt for her wasn't going to last, so

he was going to have to show her. And the only way he could
do that was by being patient, by letting time drift on and
gently showing her he hadn't changed his mind, that he still
felt the same way. And if it took a hundred years, so be it.

The next morning Alice went to bring the milk in and found
a large paper bag on the front step. A large bag that smelled
of warm, buttery croissants and fresh coffee. She picked it up
carefully and looked around. There was no sign of Cameron,
just a black car driving away, almost out of view at the corner
of the road.

There was a note inside. Short, to the point. Very Cameron.

Your verdict was correct. But I'm going to appeal...
In the meantime, please enjoy your breakfast.
When you're ready, I'll be waiting.
Cameron
x

Also very cryptic. He was going to *appeal*? What did that
mean?

An identical bag was on the step the next day, and the
next... Alice began to dread going to bring the milk in. On
the sixth day she just got angry and left it sitting outside. What
was he trying to do to her? Wear her down? Drive her insane?

If that was the plan, it was clearly working.

And she was angry with him. Very, *very* angry with him.

How dared he make her love him even more when she was
so desperately trying to get him out of her system? It just
wasn't right.

After three more days of the bag sitting on the step—and
Alice giving very strict warnings to a hopeful-looking pair of

housemates that they were dead meat if they touched it—there were no more deliveries. No more notes. No phone calls. Not even a text message. No more Cameron.

He'd given up. Just as she'd thought he would.

Now she hated him for proving her right.

Really hated him.

CHAPTER TEN

JENNIE breezed into her stepbrother's office and blew him a kiss. 'The place looks fab,' she said, then perched on the end of his desk.

Cameron dropped the folder he was holding and stood up. 'Where on earth have you been for the last month?' he bellowed.

She waved an elegant hand. 'Vegas... Here and there...'

Here and there? Give him strength! She'd abandoned him when she was supposed to be helping him with a key point in his career, and now she just wafted back in here as if nothing had happened? And what about this whole *eloping* thing? He'd been so worried about her he'd even toyed with the idea of hiring private detectives to find her. But she seemed fine to him—sitting on the edge of his desk, squashing a report from the marketing department. More than fine. He wasn't sure if he wanted to drag her into a bear hug or wring her neck.

Brotherly concern triumphed over outrage. He circled the desk and came to stand in front of her, looked her over for any sign that something was wrong.

'You're okay? Nothing's the matter?'

She gave him a bright smile. 'Absolutely fine. Haven't you noticed the wonderful tan? Got it in Acapulco.'

That was so Jennie. He'd been worried about her emotional well-being and she thought a great tan was evidence enough that things were all right. He gave her a rough squeeze and found he couldn't let go. She might drive him insane, but he was really glad to have her back.

She laughed into his ear. 'Hey! Are you okay, Cam? You're on the verge of turning python here...'

'Sorry,' he mumbled, and loosened his grasp. After giving her a gruff kiss on the top of her head, he stepped away.

Jennie narrowed her eyes and looked at him. Despite her flighty nature, she could be horribly perceptive sometimes. He decided to sidetrack her, as he didn't want a whole barrage of questions about the ball. Questions about the ball might lead to questions about Alice, and he wasn't sure he wouldn't give himself away.

After more than a week of coffee and croissants he'd realised that even that had been *pushing*, and he'd stopped. But doing nothing was killing him—even though Alice had made it clear she needed space. He was fed up with spending all day thinking about her, so when a thought popped into his head, providing a distraction, he latched onto it and looked his step-sister in the eye.

'So...where's this guy, then?'

She blinked innocently at him. 'What guy?'

He could still rethink the whole neck-wringing idea...

'The one you married?' he said, with just a tiny trace of impatience in his voice.

For a second Jennie looked bleak, and then the bright smile was back in place. She made a dismissive noise and gave him a delicate shove in the chest.

'Don't tell me you bought *that* old chestnut!' Then she started to laugh—right about the same time as Cameron's blood pressure began to rise. 'Really, Cam, you take things so literally sometimes!'

'Jen,' he said through clenched teeth, 'a message on my voicemail saying, "Sorry, hon. I'm off to Vegas to get married", combined with your sudden disappearance, would tend to make a man think that way.'

'Something's up with you, Cameron Hunter, and I want to know what it is.' It seemed he wasn't the only one who was good at using distraction techniques. She hopped off the desk and eyed him suspiciously. 'You've gone all soft and mushy.'

Hah! Soft and mushy? Try telling that to Stephanie. He'd been so unbearable in the last week that he almost expected to find her hiding under her desk every time he walked past it.

'It's Alice, isn't it?'

What…? When…? How did she *do* that? How did she see into his brain and know the things nobody else could see? He could have understood it if they'd been twins, or something, but they weren't even blood relations!

'I hear she did a good job in my stead—that you worked very closely together.'

The smile was sweet as honey. It was the one she used when she thought she might be pushing things just a little bit too far.

'I always thought she'd be much better for you than the likes of Jessica Fairly-Loves-Herself, or whatever her name is. So…' She leant forward and her voice dropped to a whisper. 'How are things going between you and the lovely Alice?'

Cameron flexed his knuckles.

'That well, huh?' she said in a dry tone. 'What did you do?'

He walked round his desk and dropped into his chair. 'I didn't do anything. I'm still not doing anything…' He launched into a bullet-pointed rundown of the whole sorry affair while Jen pulled up a chair and for once looked sympathetic, instead of like Little Miss Know-It-All.

'She says she wants to be someone's first choice,' he said finally.

Jennie reached across and stroked his arm. 'Nice cufflinks,' she said, looking down at where his sleeves protruded from his jacket. 'Unusual stones.'

He just nodded. He hadn't worn anything else since the night of the ball.

Jennie's voice was low and soft. '*Is* she your first choice?'

Cameron clamped his jaw together and nodded one more time.

'Oh, Cam,' she whispered, and came round behind him to give him a hug over the top of his office chair.

He stared into space and tried not to let the pain show in his voice. 'Seems I'm not hers, though.'

Jennie's arms squeezed a little tighter. 'I bet you are. In fact I've become a bit of a gambler since my break in Vegas, and I'd lay good money on it. You just need to prove it to her.'

He rolled his eyes. 'I've tried that.'

Jennie let go and gave him a soft clip round the head.

'Ow!'

'Not *your* way, you daft man! I could have told you *that* wouldn't work.' She walked over to the window and stared out into the atrium. 'Hmm. I might just have an idea, though— although it'll take a little setting up…'

Cameron put his head in his hands.

God help him.

Three weeks after the fashion show Alice and Coreen signed a lease for the first ever Coreen's Closet boutique. Initially they'd been interested in one of the tiny shops that fringed Greenwich Market, and one had become available. It seemed that thirty pounds apiece for frilly white baby clothes that would ultimately get covered in pureed carrot had not been Annabel's best business idea. Her children's clothes shop had closed down a few days after the Orion ball.

The success of the auction that night had been astounding. Coreen and Alice had been inundated with e-mails and phone calls, asking when and where they were going to be selling their merchandise. People seemed happy to part with obscene amounts of money if the label or the fabric was right.

They were now going to open their shop on College Approach, one of the roads in central Greenwich that surrounded the market and was full of chic little boutiques. The plan was to still keep a section of the shop that appealed to their loyal market customers—funky retro clothes for good prices—but to expand the high-end section of the business, stocking designer labels from yesteryear and becoming a place serious collectors and fashionistas would seek out.

After they'd signed all the paperwork, Coreen convinced Alice to go for a drink in one of the local cafés. 'Who cares if it's only one o'clock in the afternoon?' she said. They'd done it! Gladys and Glynis need never fear the elements again!

Alice smiled and nodded, even though she didn't really feel like it.

All her dreams had come true. She'd left her IT business behind, passing it on to a friend of a friend who was happy to pick up new clients, and she was starting a new chapter in her life. One where she was her own boss, where every day would be filled with fabulous clothes, glitz and glamour. That was what she told herself every hour on the hour, anyway. Sooner or later it would work, and she would cheer up and remember how happy she was.

The café was busy—a favourite with local office workers on a Friday lunchtime—but under the hum of conversation there was a tone, a hint of a voice she recognised. She turned from where she was sitting on a stool at the bar, waiting for her table, and scanned the room. Just as she found the face she recognised, he turned to look at her.

She hadn't seen Paul in months, and despite the fact she'd been really sore that he'd dumped her she'd hardly even thought about him during the last few weeks. He gave her a nervous smile. Alice's gaze drifted a little to the right and she saw why. The dark-haired girl he was sitting with must be Felicity. It was hardly an easy situation.

But, to be honest, she really wasn't bothered.

Paul leaned towards his new girlfriend—well, his *old* girlfriend, really—and said something in a hushed voice. She glanced up at Alice, then nodded at Paul, and kept a sharp eye on him as he got up and headed for where she was sitting at the bar.

'Hi, Al.'

She smiled at him and discovered she didn't even have to fake it. 'Hi, Paul. How are you doing?'

He shot a nervous glance back at his table. 'Oh, you know. Fine.'

Alice looked him up and down. Nope. She couldn't remember what she'd seen in him. Not that he wasn't okay-looking, in a very ordinary sort of way.

'You look different,' he said. 'Nice.'

Did he *have* to have that faint edge of surprise in his voice? She did look nice today. Ever since she'd had to think about nicer clothes to wear to Cameron's office she seemed to have discovered her own style—the old, comfortable clothes she loved mixed with a bit of vintage. Today she was even smarter than that, having had official business to attend to. She wore a forest-green jacket and a full knee-length skirt with a large funky floral print. Coreen had even produced a pair of green shoes from her famous wardrobe to match the jacket.

Paul squinted and rubbed the bridge of his nose. She'd found that quite endearing once.

'I…uh…just wanted to check there were no…uh…hard feelings.'

Something struck Alice, and she decided she did want one last thing from Paul after all. 'Paul?'

'Uh-huh?'

'Do you mind if I ask you something?'

He looked at her suspiciously. 'Depends what it is.'

How did she put this without sounding too nosey—or scary?

'Why did you decide to go back to Felicity? Really?'

Paul shuffled a little, and she could tell he was just about to say something very neutral to placate her.

'Come on, Paul. You owe me at least this.'

He pulled a face and looked over his shoulder at Felicity. 'I suppose I do.'

When he looked back at Alice she sensed he'd lost all notion of palming her off with a platitude.

'Well…I don't quite know how to say this without feeling a bit mean.'

She waved a hand. 'Honestly, I don't mind. Just spit it out.'

He blinked. 'It's not just your clothes you've changed, is it? Well, okay… You're a great girl, Al, really nice and everything. But you never once looked at me the way *she* looks at me.'

'Oh.' That wasn't what she'd been expecting at all. 'How *does* she look at you?'

Paul looked over at his girlfriend again. He caught her eye, and instantly Alice saw her whole face soften and come alive.

'Like she means it,' he said, without looking back.

Like she means it.

Alice couldn't get Paul's words out of her head. Late that night she lay awake in bed and tried to make sense of them. She thought of the way Felicity had looked at Paul. Had she never even once shone like that when *she'd* looked at him?

No. No, she hadn't.

Because she'd never felt that deeply for Paul, never felt he was her sun, moon and stars the way Felicity obviously did. She'd never felt that way about any of the men she'd been out with, not even with Tim, her first real serious relationship. She'd been devastated when he'd gone off with one of her friends without so much as an apology. But when she thought back on it now it seemed more that the rejection had stung rather than losing the man himself. After Tim she'd lowered her expectations, decided to play in her own league.

But that hadn't helped either. They'd still left. And for the first time Alice considered that maybe she'd had something to do with that.

What if all of them, like Paul, had sensed that she'd *settled* for them? Because she had. She'd only been fooling herself when she'd pretended she hadn't. They hadn't been the fantasy, but they'd been attainable—or so she'd thought. She'd kidded herself that it had been good enough, close enough to love to last. Only she hadn't fooled anyone but herself. Without exception her ex-boyfriends had moved on to girls who thought they were 'the one'. Some of them were even married with kids now.

At the time she'd just thought they were rats who'd gone

where the grass was greener, but perhaps she'd been uncharitable. At least all but Tim had been decent enough to break up with her *before* they'd started something with the new women in their lives. Maybe they'd just fallen in love and then realised that their undemanding, safe relationship with Alice wasn't all it had been cracked up to be.

She didn't grieve for the loss of any of them. Not any more.

But Cameron was a different matter.

She'd loved him. Still did. He was the one man who, when she looked at him, she meant it. And she'd sent him away. Too scared to see if maybe he meant it too.

While she'd stayed in her safe little bubble, being baggy-jumpered Alice who nobody ever looked at twice, she'd had hope. Hope that maybe she had the potential to be more, the potential to be really loved. But if she'd tried—stripped off all her defences and really tried—and Cameron had still moved on, then she'd have been crushed, knowing that if it didn't happen with him it wouldn't happen with anyone.

Had she hardened herself too much? Pushed him away too hard?

If he'd kept on sending her breakfast she might have had had the courage to ring him up right now, no matter what time it was. But the croissants and warm coffee had stopped coming, and she had no idea what he felt or what he was doing now. If she really wanted to find out she was going to have to dig up some strength from somewhere.

I'll be waiting…

The line from Cameron's note replaced Paul's words on the loop in her head.

Was it too late? Was he still waiting? Suddenly she really needed to know.

* * *

Coreen's voice was so loud that Alice had to hold her mobile phone away from her ear.

'You need to get your butt up to the V&A, pronto. They've got a new exhibit in the fashion collection. It's fabulous—right up your street—and there's a little drinks thing and a private showing tonight, before it goes on public display tomorrow. Just give your name at the side entrance and they'll let you in.'

Alice had wondered where Coreen had been all afternoon, and now it was all starting to make sense. Until the shop opened just after Christmas they were continuing to run Coreen's Closet as an open-air enterprise. Monday was their day off after all the weekend markets. Personally, she'd already spent a long afternoon doing absolutely nothing, and could really use a distraction from staring out of the window and thinking about Cameron.

She'd composed an e-mail to him ten times. She'd deleted it ten times.

Perhaps these things needed to be said in person. In that case she'd have to wait until tomorrow and see if she could wangle an appointment out of Stephanie.

Her heart went into overdrive at the thought. What if she'd been right? What if Cameron had moved on to someone else? Someone even more elegant and stunning than Jessica—if that were possible.

'Erm…*hello*? Earth to Alice!'

Alice jumped. 'Sorry! Just drifted off for a bit. Thinking about this V&A thing…'

'Of *course* that's what you were thinking about.' Coreen didn't sound convinced.

Alice decided to ignore the sarcasm and talk clothes. They'd rehashed the whole Cameron thing so many times now that even Alice was getting sick of hearing herself talk about it.

'What will people be wearing?'

'Pff! People…Who cares what anyone else is wearing? But vintage would be a good choice, given the opportunity to mingle with like-minded people.'

Alice picked up a stack of the business cards they'd had printed for the new shop. At least her professional life was going right; it was only her love life that had disappeared down the drain.

'I know,' Coreen said. 'The little blue mini-dress. The one with the matching jacket.'

It was a good choice, but Alice had something else in mind. It was high time she listened to her instincts and learned to choose outfits without Coreen's input. Coreen might sulk about that for a bit, but she had known this day would come. In the end she'd be pleased to see her protégé had spread her wings and learned to fly.

The Christmas lights were twinkling as Alice stepped out of South Kensington tube station. There was a Victorian tiled underpass that led to the cluster of museums situated on and around Cromwell Road, but she'd decided on fresh air instead. It was seven o'clock on a clear night. Alice hadn't needed to check opening times or consult a map. Her grandmother had brought her to the Victoria and Albert museum many times as a child, and she'd loved to see all the fabulous jewellery, the things from far-flung places around the globe and the massive sculptures.

The fashion collection, specialising in *haute couture* down the decades, had always been a draw. Maybe that was why she'd fallen in love with the whole vintage clothing scene when she'd stumbled across it. She and Gran had spent ages inspecting each dress carefully, picking out which ones were their favourites and settling on the one that they'd wear to a ball, if they ever got the chance.

Alice sighed.

Would her dress be all right? Suddenly she was second-guessing her choice of a cute little short-sleeved dress, with its wide panels of black satin dotted with pink roses at the waist and hem. Was it a little too much? Well, too late now to run home and hide away in a baggy fleece. She'd just have to brave it out.

She ignored the grand entrance and made her way to a smaller one at the side of the building in Exhibition Road. A security guard merely smiled at her and waved her on as she walked through the revolving doors and told him why she was there.

Her destination was only a short distance from the entrance, down a flight of marble stairs, just off a long hall full of sculptures. Her heels clipped on the mosaic floor as she passed headless and armless statues, all male torsos, rippling with muscles and leashed strength. That made her sigh too. Why did everything remind her of Cameron? And she hadn't even seen him without his shirt off.

The only thing visible at the wide entrance to the fashion exhibit was a long, horizontal display case filled with shoes—embroidered seventeenth-century court shoes, buttoned boots in deep red leather, and sequined platforms all stood proudly side by side.

As she climbed the few steps to the entrance she slowed down. If this was a preview, with cocktails and canapés, where were all the people? Why couldn't she hear them talking or glasses clinking? Perhaps Coreen had got the time wrong. Perhaps she was early.

Her hunch was borne out by the fact that, apart from the lone guard she could still see on duty by the entrance there wasn't a soul in the place. She glanced at him, wondering if it was really all right to enter the room and go exploring, but he just nodded and gave her a little wink.

Although the vintage clothes were all housed in a vast domed room, it always felt very close, very intimate, because the lighting was kept deliberately low to preserve the wonderful fabrics. The central part of the room was closed off, only used for special exhibitions, but the main collection could be seen by walking the perimeter—long glass cases on each side of the walkway, displaying clothes of all kinds on headless white mannequins.

She'd never been here at night before, but far from being creepy, the added depth to the darkness only made the exhibits seem even brighter and more wonderful, each one illuminated by a soft spotlight. It was almost too good to be true to be here on her own, with no one to crowd her view, no one to hurry her along.

Well, okay, then. If she was early, she was going to make the most of it and take her time. She'd probably never have this opportunity again. Keeping an ear out for anyone else arriving, she started to circle the room, stopping every now and then to pay special attention to some of her favourite pieces—a shocking pink fifties ballgown with a stiff skirt, a 'flapper' dress in swirling silk with sequins and jewels and a court mantua, all creamy satin and exquisite embroidery.

At each 'corner' of the circular room there was a curved alcove where the display cases made a C-shape. A large octagonal glass case stood in the extra space. The first she'd passed had housed an embroidered Regency wedding dress. She approached the second octagonal case with curiosity. This must be it—the new exhibit. Only she couldn't see what was inside properly because the lights were out. She walked towards it, trying to make out what it was...

A dress of some kind, in a dark shiny fabric.

When she was just a few steps away the small spotlights in the ceiling of the case started to glow, shining brighter and brighter until there was no doubt as to what it contained.

Her dress. Her dark green bias-cut Elsa Schiaparelli dress. It said so on the card—even mentioned her name as the person who had donated it.

And her shoes.

Beside the dress, at the bottom of the case on a specially created stand, lit so the Lucite heels sparkled and glimmered, were her shoes. She crouched down and inspected the heel of the left shoe. She would never have known it had been snapped off if she hadn't been the one to do the snapping.

But...

The silence in the darkened gallery thickened. Alice held her breath and slowly straightened. Someone was here with her. But she didn't turn round yet; her brain was working overtime. The only person it could be—the only way to explain all of this was if it was...

Suddenly her eyes adjusted. The dress and the shoes blurred away and a reflection in the glass came into focus.

Cameron. Standing behind her.

Looking at her as if he meant it.

She spun around, still unable to breathe. He didn't move, just continued to let his eyes wander over her. Somehow he didn't look a bit like the Cameron she'd come to know again in recent weeks, but more as she recalled him from the past. He wasn't even wearing a suit. Just jeans and a long-sleeved T-shirt.

The clothes were just a symptom. As she stared back at him, remembering to squeeze and release her lungs, forcing air into them, she saw the real transformation. All the layers had been peeled away and he seemed younger, more vulnerable. His eyes, far from being blank and unreadable, were telling her all kinds of things. Things she could hardly dare to believe.

'You said you wanted an ordinary guy…' He shrugged. 'I think I've found you one.'

She shook her head. He would never be ordinary, and she didn't want him to be. He was Cameron. *Her* Cameron. A perfect fit.

But in another way what he'd said wasn't too far off the mark. He wasn't an untouchable god or an out-of-reach prince. He was just a man, with all his faults and flaws and fears.

And how she loved him.

He must have seen something of that in her eyes, because he stepped forward, more determined now, and ran his hands down her bare arms. After weeks of being deprived of his touch it was all that was needed to blast any remaining defences away.

'You're not perfect,' he stated slowly, a smile starting at the corners of his mouth.

'Not being very romantic here, Cameron…'

He laughed softly and pressed a kiss to her forehead. 'I don't want you to be perfect. I just want you to be you.' His lips didn't stop there, and he placed tiny kisses along her temple, across her cheekbone. 'Because I'm not perfect either, and I'm finally okay with that concept. I don't need to prove myself to anyone who will take notice any more.'

She wound her arms around his waist and pulled him closer. He didn't need to explain—she got it. They were both incomplete, stupid, and very, very human. And thank heaven for that, she thought, as he slid his hands around her waist and held her tighter still.

'I don't care if you're perfect or not,' she said. 'You're my Gilbert after all.'

His lips had been poised to place a kiss at the edge of her jaw and he paused for a fraction of a second. 'Your *what*?'

'Never mind,' she whispered back. 'Just shut up and kiss me.'

She decided she liked it very much when control-hungry Cameron stopped being habitually stubborn and did as he was told. She liked it very much.

It was such a relief, such a joy to be here with him, that she felt tears collect in her lashes. 'I'm sorry I pushed you away,' she said, her voice scratchy. 'I couldn't understand why you of all people would decide to keep me—the second-hand girl that everyone else had discarded.'

He kept her pressed up against him, but leaned back a little so he could focus on her face.

'Oh, I'm planning on keeping you for a long time—as long as you promise to keep me back. You're the best thing in my lousy life, Alice, because you challenge me to be the best man I can be. Because you demand it of me. And up until now I've been too afraid to be that man.'

'Shh,' she said, pressing her fingertips to his lips, feeling her tears fall.

He shook his head gently to dislodge her fingers and they fell away. 'No, it's true.' His gaze softened and her breath caught. It was as if he'd just reached out and dived inside her. 'I'm going to keep you because you love me, Alice Morton...'

That was also true. And no amount of running away was ever going to change that.

'You love me the way I love you,' he said. 'With everything I can give—good, bad and in between. You've got it all.'

And he bent forward to deliver the sweetest kiss yet, one that made the room spin and her feet tingle. Alice kissed him right back, sensing in some way that they were marking each other as the other one's property. Finally she could let herself pour everything into her kiss, with no fear barring her from giving everything she had in return.

As always, they managed to say a lot of what they wanted to say, resolve a lot of things, without the need for words at all. Alice gave a deep, heartfelt, happy sigh and steadied herself against the glass display case. She was feeling decidedly wobbly.

'I'm glad you rescued my shoes,' she said, glancing away from him for only a second. 'They look happy here. I don't think they would have stood up to twenty-first-century abuse. I'd have hated to see them ruined.'

He smiled. 'And the dress? Do you want it back? I'll get it for you if—'

She shook her head and kissed his neck, right where his pulse was beating, and felt a surge of power at the shuddering response it produced in him.

'I'm glad about that too.' She smiled up at him. 'Anyway, I don't think I need it any more.'

His smile grew into a wide grin.

'I was hoping you'd say that, because I have another dress in mind. I don't care what style it is, whether it's new or old, but I do have one stipulation…'

She chuckled. 'You're not going to go all *Cameron* on me again now you've got what you want, are you?'

A flash of the old arrogance returned. 'Of course I am. You wouldn't have me any other way.'

He was right. Who would want anything but this wonderful, determined, romantic, *thick-headed* man? He was definitely a keeper. She lifted onto her tiptoes and kissed him. She seemed to be doing a lot of that tonight. Oh, well…

Then she realised she'd been sidetracked and pulled away. 'What sort of stipulation?'

She'd expected him to laugh, but he pulled her close and breathed into her ear in a rough voice. 'Like I said… I don't mind if it's long or short, fancy or plain, old or new. Just as long as it's white. And I have to warn you, it comes with matching jewellery.' Suddenly he got all serious, took a few deep breaths. 'That means I'm asking you to marry me, if you hadn't worked that out yet.'

Alice threw her head back and laughed. He didn't do *subtle*, did he, this man of hers? When she stopped laughing, he was looking puzzled.

'That's a *yes*, if you hadn't worked it out yet.' She smoothed his forehead flat with the pads of her thumbs. 'But I have a stipulation too.'

A flash of fear glittered in his eyes and she kissed it away.

'Don't make that face, Cameron. Can't you see this look?' She paused and let her eyes do the talking. 'This is the look of a girl who's fallen in love and isn't about to fall out again.'

Cameron answered her with a delicious kiss, and as he pulled her closer still she whispered in his ear. 'I love you, Cameron Hunter. But about this jewellery… Let's be clear about one thing—I'm not wearing a tiara for anybody. Not even you.'

He just laughed, picked her up, and waltzed her round the empty gallery.

We'll be spotlighting a different series
every month throughout 2009
to celebrate our 60th anniversary.

Look for Silhouette® Nocturne™ in October!

Travel through time to experience tales
that reach the boundaries of life and death.
Bestselling authors Lindsay McKenna, Cindy
Dees, P.C. Cast and Merline Lovelace join
together in a brand-new, four-book
Time Raiders miniseries.

TIME RAIDERS

REQUEST YOUR FREE BOOKS!
2 FREE NOVELS PLUS 2
FREE GIFTS!

HARLEQUIN *Romance*®

From the Heart, For the Heart

YES! Please send me 2 FREE Harlequin® Romance novels and my 2 FREE gifts (gifts are worth about $10). After receiving them, if I don't wish to receive any more books, I can return the shipping statement marked "cancel". If I don't cancel, I will receive 4 brand-new novels every month and be billed just $3.84 per book in the U.S. or $4.24 per book in Canada. That's a savings of at least 15% off the cover price! It's quite a bargain! Shipping and handling is just 50¢ per book.* I understand that accepting the 2 free books and gifts places me under no obligation to buy anything. I can always return a shipment and cancel at any time. Even if I never buy another book, the two free books and gifts are mine to keep forever.

114 HDN EYU3 314 HDN EYKG

Name	(PLEASE PRINT)

Address	Apt. #

City	State/Prov.	Zip/Postal Code

Signature (if under 18, a parent or guardian must sign)

Mail to the **Harlequin Reader Service:**
IN U.S.A.: P.O. Box 1867, Buffalo, NY 14240-1867
IN CANADA: P.O. Box 609, Fort Erie, Ontario L2A 5X3

Not valid to current subscribers of Harlequin Romance books.

**Are you a subscriber of Harlequin Romance books
and want to receive the larger-print edition?
Call 1-800-873-8635 today!**

* Terms and prices subject to change without notice. Prices do not include applicable taxes. Sales tax applicable in N.Y. Canadian residents will be charged applicable provincial taxes and GST. Offer not valid in Quebec. This offer is limited to one order per household. All orders subject to approval. Credit or debit balances in a customer's account(s) may be offset by any other outstanding balance owed by or to the customer. Please allow 4 to 6 weeks for delivery. Offer available while quantities last.

Your Privacy: Harlequin Books is committed to protecting your privacy. Our Privacy Policy is available online at www.eHarlequin.com or upon request from the Reader Service. From time to time we make our lists of customers available to reputable third parties who may have a product or service of interest to you. If you would prefer we not share your name and address, please check here. ☐

HR09R

HARLEQUIN *Romance*

Coming Next Month

Available October 13, 2009

Look for the second books in both Marion Lennox's royal trilogy and Barbara Hannay's baby duet, plus makeovers, miracles and marriage, come to Harlequin® Romance!

#4123 THE FRENCHMAN'S PLAIN-JANE PROJECT Myrna Mackenzie
In Her Shoes...
Bookish and shy, Meg longs to be poised and confident. There's more than a simple makeover in store when she's hired by seductive Frenchman Etienne!

#4124 BETROTHED: TO THE PEOPLE'S PRINCE Marion Lennox
The *Marrying His Majesty* miniseries continues.
Nikos is the people's prince, but the crown belongs to the reluctant Princess Athena, whom he was forbidden to marry. He must convince her to come home....

#4125 THE GREEK'S LONG-LOST SON Rebecca Winters
Escape Around the World
Self-made millionaire Theo can have anything his heart desires. But there's just one thing he wants—his first love, Stella, and their long-lost son.

#4126 THE BRIDESMAID'S BABY Barbara Hannay
Baby Steps to Marriage...
In the conclusion to this miniseries, unresolved feelings resurface as old friends Will and Lucy are thrown together as best man and bridesmaid. But a baby is the last thing they expect.

#4127 A PRINCESS FOR CHRISTMAS Shirley Jump
Christmas Treats
Secret princess Mariabella won't let anyone spoil her seaside haven. So when hotshot property developer Jake arrives, she'll stand up to all gorgeous six feet of him!

#4128 HIS HOUSEKEEPER BRIDE Melissa James
Heart to Heart
Falling for the boss wasn't part of Sylvie's job description. But Mark's sad eyes intrigue her and his smile makes her melt. Before she knows it, this unassuming housekeeper's in over her head!

HRCNMBPA0909